D1347221

Abigail Tarttelin is a writer and actress. Her novel *Golden Boy* received a 2014 Alex Award and was a finalist for the 2014 Lambda Literary Award. She lives in London. *Flick* is her debut novel. Find out more at AbigailTarttelin.com and on Twitter @abigailsbrain.

By Abigail Tarttelin

Flick
Golden Boy

Praise for *Golden Boy*

'*Golden Boy* is terrific. A poignant, brave and important book'
  S. J. Watson, bestselling author of *Before I Go to Sleep*

'[Tarttelin] is a natural storyteller'
            Matt Haig, bestselling author of *The Humans*

'Gripping and beautifully written, Abigail Tarttelin's *Golden Boy* is a courageous and profound exploration of social and sexual identity and its world of manifold complexities and challenges'
Sahar Delijani, author of *Children of the Jacaranda Tree*

'Abigail Tarttelin is a fearless writer. In *Golden Boy*, she balances a harrowing coming of age with a deeply compassionate portrait of a family in crisis, and the result is sometimes brutal, often tender, and always compelling. This is a gripping and fully-realized novel'
        Emily St John Mandel, author of *Station Eleven*

'Gripping' *Cosmopolitan*

'An original read about a young person in an extraordinary situation . . . Unlike anything you will have read before . . . Brave, unique and utterly compelling. This is a book that will certainly make you think about life'
                    Heat magazine

'Tarttelin broaches the topic of intersexuality bravely, describes the crimes committed against Max intensely, and evokes his ensuing emotions poignantly. A highly praised new author, her fresh, modern approach and contemporary writing style result in an inimitably of-the-moment novel which is beautifully matter-of-fact, eloquently meditative and fearlessly action-packed, all at once' *We Love This Book*

'*Golden Boy* is undeniably one of the most incredible books I have ever read . . . Such an important novel, one I wish everyone would read, one I feel should be read in schools. It's perfect, and I am so, so glad I've had the opportunity to read it'

www.onceuponabookcase.co.uk

FLICK

ABIGAIL TARTTELIN

WEIDENFELD & NICOLSON

A W&N PAPERBACK

First published in Great Britain in 2011
by Beautiful Books
This paperback edition published in 2015
by Weidenfeld & Nicolson,
an imprint of Orion Books Ltd,
Carmelite House, 50 Victoria Embankment,
London, EC4Y 0DZ

An Hachette UK Company

1 3 5 7 9 10 8 6 4 2

A CIP catalogue record for this book
is available from the British Library.

ISBN 978-1-7802-2517-3

Typeset by Input Data Services Ltd, Bridgwater, Somerset

Printed and Bound in Great Britain by Clays Ltd, St Ives plc

The Orion Publishing Group's policy is to use papers that
are natural, renewable and recyclable products and made
from wood grown in sustainable forests. The logging and
manufacturing processes are expected to conform to the
environmental regulations of the country of origin.

www.orionbooks.co.uk

This story should be read while playing *We'll Live and Die In These Towns* by The Enemy.

PART ONE

I

The Night Before

'Fuck me.'

Ashley's voice echoes up out of the darkness. I lie stretched out on her single bed while beside me on the floor her bare knees part, close and part again in an attempt to lure me into her frequently visited pants. This is Friday night, always has been. Ash throws her neediness and tits in my face, I remove my revulsion and dick from her reach and our friendship teeters along unchanging, which is kind of sweet when you think about it. But it's also inevitable, considering we've lived in the same crescent in Osford for all my fifteen years, til Ash moved to the centre of Langrick on her sixteenth two months ago. Langrick's a mile south of Osford by the way. She dreams big, does Ash.

She moans, I'm guessing she thinks it's seductive, and I shudder. Jesus. *If,* and this is purely theoretical, but *if* I did succumb to Ash's few charms, bang her and risk getting her pregnant, Ash wouldn't think twice about keeping it and that's enough to put me right off. 'Cause then our poor bastard-child would grow up within the same five-mile radius that we have, and some girl would one day rub up against him and try to tempt him with month-old Jack-Daniel's-and-fag breath. It's the circle of life. In any case with the amount of lads who've climbed through Ash's 'shop door' it must be pretty disease-ridden by now. Harsh but probably true. Sex is so political when you're underage.

Ash lifts one leg in the air and scratches down it with her bubblegum-pink nails. I look at my dick to check for signs of weakness – no response. Good man.

'Flick? . . . Fuck me. I'm waiting,' she singsongs in that teasing 'I'm-a-little-schoolgirl-check-out-my-knee-socks-and-pleated-skirt-but-you'll-never-touch-me' way she talks to older men. What a bitch. If she didn't have a tight ass and cute tits and if we (meaning our mates) didn't all go to the same nursery school, most of us wouldn't even talk to her, but Ash never reeled me in. She's a slut, but at the same time she's like a child, every weekend crying over some guy who doesn't love her, playing out the same my-daddy-left-me routine over and over again as if she was six years old and it was yesterday. And I'm no paedophile. That said, Ash doesn't have that much to complain about. Her parents still fuck, so the sentiment's there.

'Flick?' More silence. She blows the hair out of her face, a big, bouncy and admittedly beautiful brown Afro, and giggles, and by the sound of her voice I can tell she's grinning in a sleepy, stoned way. 'You're totally wasted.'

'Yeah, Ash, I'm completely gone,' I deadpan, getting up off the bed. She lies on the stained shag-rug in her diamante clasp bra, Scooby Doo T-shirt and black G-string. I have to step over her to get out of the door and narrowly miss her hand swiping for my dick.

'Hey, Flick, I'll take your virginity if you like, then you can fuck who you want.'

'Maybe next week, Ash.'

I worm my way around ten conked-out bodies in the living room, pick up a joint, suck it, put it down, jump down the stairs, and I'm out the door of the flat and onto the road. Walking home at night is my favourite part of the whole Friday at Ashley's debacle. No longer do I have to

4

talk bollocks or avoid rape. I am free. It is cold and smells fresh and all I can hear are the waves breaking on the sand, a quarter of a mile east.

The walk up to where I live in Osford from Ash's dingy place in Langrick is practically silent but for the sound of the water. It's always like this on this stretch of coast at night, in a part of England dimly visible just beyond the bright lights of seaside tourist spots, and lacking the pull of a rollercoaster or a Maccy Ds. I skip along like a ponce, hands in pockets, on desolate, isolated, particularly creepy marshland with not a tree in sight, watching out for the only people you ever see out at this time: night fishermen and young, horny couples. Langrick is a quiet market town, tattered, the fishing industry gone, and the whole place way past its best, with a haggard and aged population living in pebble-dashed buildings that get progressively shitter the further you get out from the centre. On the other hand, it's where our school is, and more importantly where the pubs will turn a blind eye to underage drinking, so our social life exists within Langrick's narrow alleys, its empty car parks and the smell of battered fish.

To the north, Osford is its suburbia, a sprawl of 90s-built semis and terraces with jazzy tiles and 'family friendly' neighbourhoods, where all the windows overlook the streets, so nosy old birds and lonely pervs can hawk-eye me and my mates when we're hanging out. Not sure that was the paradise intended by the town planners back in the day. Both towns are almost too tiny for the word but, along with a string of new housing estates and old villages along the North East coast, they make up Clyde County, an area whose jurisdiction has been fought over, passed about, and now forgotten and left to rot by successive local governments who didn't want to pay for it – for us. We're not classy and in demand, like London. We're sort of grubby and old-fashioned, and tacked on to the top of North Yorkshire.

Clyde's place names all come from a long tradition of Norwegian settlers coming here for land and the fishing opportunities, which is why the names sound like we're in Svalbard and everyone looks Scandinavian. Learnt that one day when I was paying attention in Geography. It doesn't happen often, 'cause Miss P's tits are epic.

Suddenly there's a dip in the sand dunes next to me, and the salty April air buffets my cheeks and I breathe in, deep and clean, and stop momentarily, halted by the awesome enormity of the landscape and that feeling you get when there aren't houses or lights around and it's just you and nature and it occurs to you that this is forever, that if you lived in forever, this is what it would be like.

I've grown up by the North Sea, and my proximity to this vast and constant guardian makes me forget at times that life is so transient and ultimately (although this might not be everyone's opinion, it's mine) meaningless. I run towards the whispering waves, I stand on the sands in the dark, the ground sinks beneath my trainers as the water draws back and everything connects for just a second. Otherwise, it's pretty shite.

My name is Flick and these are my images of my disconnected life, my forgettable weeks and unforgettable weekends. I am one of the disaffected youth, a child of the ASBO generation and we live like we might die every second, while missing all the real things we should be living for (it's true, we know what we lack – why d'you think we're wankered half the time?). These few lines, this poem to post-pubescence details one stand-out summer in my life when, and I kid you not, I suffered two epiphanies, two real things that I learnt.

The first was the name of the (possible) love of my life, the second, about myself – I realised I was a knobend. And what a wonderful thing to learn at the tender age of fifteen. The only other need-to-know detail is that I am so-called Flick, because my life is like the pages of a flick-book – a series of fast and frenetic images, delivered in double time, a bit of humour, a dash of tragedy, fairly black and white in its lack of variety – the end ever approaching as the pages run out. Each page a story, each flick a life failing. A life in bright, yet entirely similar images. A life ending fast. A life in snap-shots. So, for your pleasure, here's a few of them.

I'll start from where I left off. So I'm back from the waves, salt crusted on the hem of my jeans, and I'm walking along the promenade, taking in the sea air, and thinking that, while I'm always the first to disregard Ash's subtle sugges-tions (and blatant pleas), there is one point she brings up that other people seem to constantly need addressing: so yes, I am, in fact, a virgin and no, it doesn't bother me. I have a perfectly good right hand (and left for that matter) and if 'The Hits' channel is on, and there's maybe that Rihanna video playing, Farmer Palmer and his five lovely daughters are all I need for a good time, thank you very much. Ash just thinks if she mocks me enough about my pure and innocent ways – in her opinion a pain in the arse for any fifteen year old – I'll want to sleep with her. The logic is flawed because what I lack in experience I make up for in charisma, and while other lads might freak I really couldn't give a shit what she thinks. I'm laidback about it. I'd just like to lose it with some dignity. Maybe that sounds a little gay but I personally think I've been ruined by Disney like the rest of my gener-ation. Even Ash, tallying lads like she used to collect My Little Pony, thinks one day her prince will come. I guess I'm just waiting for something different. Just as I arrive on the outskirts of Osford, A shout interrupts my eloquent reverie.

'FLICK!' A yelp sounding excitedly from a parked black Peugeot 306. Some chav twat no doubt. 'FLICK! All right?'

I peer closer and a bony head on a scrawny chicken-leg-like neck sticks out of the side-window. I laugh, happy to see him, as he beams at me. 'All right, our Gav?'

Gav smiles back, a big gappy grin like a kid in a toy-shop. Gavin Culkin lives on my estate in a semi identical to ours, but his mam's been replaced by some blonde tart with a fag permanently attached to her face and they don't know where the original's skipped off to. Possibly Ness-on-Sea, the neighbour told our mam, but that's another coastal town a few miles south of us, so how they don't know where she is beats me.

'Yeah, I'm great man, how're you? You look good, you been working out haven't you, y'little bastard? Right big muscles, you'll be able to take me in a year!'

'Yeah,' I say dubiously. Gav's a skinny runt, addicted to pot and poppers and on and off smack. 'You'd better watch it.'

He grins wider.

'Get in, are you going home? Get in, mate, I'll drive ya!' Troy and Fez, local hardheads and acquaintances of Gav's, come out of the kebab house and we all climb in. In terms of personality, Gav shouts the loudest, but Fez is the undisputed leader of their gang. They're all older than me by a good six or seven years, and Gav is the only one I've actually talked to before, but it's a small part of the world and the reputation of a man like Fez precedes him.

You know those kids who are fucking nuts? Like five years old, bruised knees, maybe even a little cute to look at, but psychotic, running around at school ramming the doll's house with their skull, eating sand and punching anyone bigger than them to show them who's boss? That was Fez. Except he grew up, started in on whatever drugs were going around, got kicked out of school for stabbing a teacher with a compass and now he doesn't do much but hang about smoking, dealing, collecting Jobseeker's Allowance and starting fights. So unless I'm feeling like being bottled over the head and picking shards of glass from my hairdo, I generally steer clear of him. Still, tonight he seems pretty out of it, so I'm feeling a little cocky. I grin at Troy, as I get in the car, nodding at Fez, who sits beside me.

'Not lookin' too good, is he?'

He knows better than to grin back.

Troy is Fez's sidekick, quiet, a bit moody, and built like a brick shithouse. He's the muscle, but he doesn't start on someone unless Fez gives the say-so, as if he's just punching people for a lack of anyone better to hang out with.

Troy holds the wheel of the car and drives while Gav's shaky hands skilfully roll a joint and Fez swigs from a bottle of Bud, while waving a wrap of doner meat haphazardly in his left hand so it drips grease onto my lap. I glance at him to see if this is intentional and his narrow blue eyes glare back with a confrontational, stoned, mean look. Poor bastard hasn't got a clue.

'Hey, Flick, did you go to Nikki's on Tuesday?'

'Yeah, yeah, I did,' I say to Gav, still on the receiving end of Fez's stoned stare-out. I start to sense it's some sort of competition and if I blink or look away first Fez will be the bigger man. I do anyway. 'Everyone was there, even Pie went.'

Gav sniggers. 'Did she say anything about me?'

Fuck. Gav's got this big thing about Nikki. According to Troy, he used to sit behind her in Maths class and lick

9

her hair. The image of Gav's jittery, stringy body wanking, rabbit-like, to Nikki appears in my mind whenever he asks me about her, so I try to avoid his questions as often as possible. Urgh.

'I don't know. I didn't really talk to her that much.'

'How's your brother?' Troy asks me, with a smirk at Gav. Gav mouths 'fuck off' back.

'Yeah, he's good, he got promoted at the steelworks.'

'Yeah?'

'Yeah. He's a supervisor. He doesn't drive the forklifts and that now, he watches other people do it.'

My brother, Tommo, is married to Nikki, another reason why I find the above image fucking sick. Tommo was in Gav's year as well. They're both twenty-three and they couldn't be more different. Tommo's massive (muscle-wise, not fat, like), serious and dependable, and a little bit fascist. In many ways the perfect big brother. He doesn't do drugs, has shit taste in music and married Nikki two years ago. They live in their own semi, in a better estate than ours. Oh yeah, Tommo's moving up in the world all right, but he won't move far. He'll never leave here which means he'll be in steel his whole life and his children'll have the same grey, malnourished look all the kids who live next to the works do. Our line of coast looks deceptively like paradise if you look one way, at the slightly better sandstone townhouses of Ness, and the pier, and the cliffs. If you look the other way, past the toddlers playing in the shallows, swallowing pints of water as they learn to swim, you can see the waste from those gloomy, grey towers gushing out and bursting over the sea like smoke erupting from a volcano. I've got a half-sister as well, Dad's from a little dalliance before he met Mum. She's twenty-nine now, and we don't see her much. She turned into just as much of a slut as her mother and lives in a flat above a chippie in Sandford. Sandford's our nearest city. It's soulless, the centre having been bombed to shit in World War Two and rebuilt in crappy 1960s grey block buildings that look like a series of prisons but actually contain shops, it's mildly dangerous, and it's about an hour away by car. I don't know what my sister does, besides get abortions. Teagan, her name is. Tee to her mates.

'FLICK!'

'What?'

'I asked you a question man, where were you?' Gav giggles like a thirteen year old.

'I don't . . .' I frown. I've no clue. I admit I was off on one.

Gav leans in, Troy's on the wheel. 'D'you think Nikki would?'

'Jesus, Gav!'

'What? You can't blame a man for asking!'

'She's my sister-in-law!'

'Yeah, so you know her! What d'you think?'

'I, I don't, I . . .' I give up, 'cause what difference will it make what I tell him? He'll still get wasted next time he sees her and tell her 'I love you Nikki' with a big dope-eyed smile. 'I don't know, Gav, maybe. Ask her yourself.'

'Wicked! I will!'

'Uh huh.' My head's starting to tighten. We bump on the pavement and off again.

'Oi! You'll wreck me tyres!' Gav frowns at Troy as we drop down to road level, ash from his joint floating about the car.

'All right!' says Troy, in a heavy Clyde County tongue. 'It's just so's I know I've parked properly, close to the kerb as it said int' driving test.'

'Giz that.' I lean over and take one last long drag, holding the joint in Gav's hand.

He gives me a cheeky wink. 'Yeah, you get that down you, my son.'

I nod him thanks and back out my door, bumping it shut. Gav rolls down his window as I walk up the drive.

'See you, gorgeous!'

'Shut the fuck up,' I grin back. 'You'll wake me mam!'

And I'm in the door, up the stairs, on the bed, dead.

2

Education Aggravation

As always, the week passes by with little event. It's the run-up to our GCSEs and I'm supposed to be taking ten this summer, eleven if they don't bump me down from the top Maths set, but nothing seems to have changed in terms of workload or pressure and I'm not bothered enough to ask why. In fact, I'm worryingly not bothered. Or rather, I would be worried, but it's the very fact that I'm so not worried in any way that is so worrying (or should be, if that makes sense). So we go to classes and hang around the lockers and make the effort as far as we know how. Stuff happens and none of it means much. I get a B on a Maths test and fail a Tech one. We get a lesson on what we want to do with our lives, and no one knows, so they tell us our options, which doesn't take long. There's never any point in remembering these kind of weeks, so I spend most of my time in one of the music practice rooms with Ash and her best mate Daisy, swigging vodka and orange from a Volvic bottle and pissing about on the drums. It's easy to skive class in the music rooms because they're soundproof and no one but us really uses them, so Ash and I use them to get drunk in and flirt to our hearts' content, which I enjoy safe in the knowledge that nothing is ever going to happen between us. Usually I also spend a lot of time laughing at my own jokes while Ash paints her nails and complains about all the older boyfriends who've screwed her over, or not screwed her, or screwed her in a particularly strange fashion, like the guy who said he wanted to carry her black babies and then followed her about until she threatened to smash her face in with her wakeboard.

Daisy, far stupider than Ash and not as attractive, tells us the latest stories about her dad. Her dad's a pervert. Her sister once walked in on him photographing his girlfriend's pussy on their coffee table and last week Daisy came in one lunchtime unexpected to find her dad asleep on the couch with a rampant rabbit and a rental copy of *Bitches on Heat* next to him. Ella, another of Ash's girl gang, of which I am an honorary member, walks in on this last sentence. Ella's pretty, in a vapid way, and skinny, and talks a lot about how fat she is to anyone who'll listen.

'Oh, I've got that. Hey, there's a new family moved in next door to mine and it's a couple of dykes with a gay son and Baz says he's going to burn their house down and shout gay burn.' She says all this very sweetly and without missing a beat, like one of those dolls where you pull a string in their back and they say set phrases in a dumb blonde accent. If I could auction Ella off as a novelty amusement on eBay I'd make a fortune. She peers at Ash's school skirt, which Ash has rolled up to show two tantalising slivers of bum cheek split by a neon pink thong.

'That's a weird skirt,' Ella comments, looking at Ash.

'Why?' Ash says, with a mean grin. 'Does it make me look fat?'

I smirk involuntarily, then cover it as Ella makes an odd half-sick, half-snot noise. Ash thinks Ella's a bitch because her face is less manly than Ash's.

'Fuck you, Flick.'

'Tactless but true.' We smile heartlessly at each other and I beat out a little rhythm on the drum kit (a shit session

14

pro with plastic skins, screws missing on the toms and the bass drum kicked through. Its condition and quality says everything about our school you would ever need to know). 'What's this family like then?'

'I told you. Two dykes and a gay son. And one daughter but I didn't meet her. She was apparently talking about coming out on Friday though. One of the dykes said so.'

Ash grunts. Very attractive. 'She's not coming to mine.'

Typical. We live in a place that's so backward most English people don't know where it is. Obviously it's not surprising, considering this, that if someone's gay they get slaughtered, but I don't see the fuss myself. Everyone's a little bit gay. Ash lezzes up every weekend to get the perverts on the bar to buy her drinks. She's a classy bird, that Ash.

Ella blinks dazedly at us. 'The girl's called Rainbow.'

'RAINBOW?'

Miss Clark, the music teacher, sixty-plus and a spinster, smells of piss, literally your walking stereotype, sticks her head in the door at this point (nosy bitch) and whines over our laughter.

'Can we *stop* this *noise*?'

She's drowned out by Ash bursting out with another shout of 'RAINBOW!!' at which I drunkenly giggle.

'Get *out, pleeease*!'

'All right, all right, we're leaving.' I grab Ash's hand and we head for the back field, behind the pavilion. Time for a spliff.

3

Kicking the Bucket

Smoke rises around my face and I'm drifting away on it, dreaming in colours, floating on feathers. A hot pulsing wave moves up through my body, beating in my groin, warming my stomach, caressing my chest like the finely manicured hands of a high-class hooker (or so I imagine). I feel it pushing from inside my face on my cheeks and the back of my eyes, numbing my features, clouding my expression, and finally, flawlessly, curling deliciously and airily around my brain (or lack thereof). I giggle indulgently, hornily and smoke shoots up past my eyes to the ceiling, billowing out of my mouth. It's called having a bucket, and by participating in this equally social and antisocial act we, the participants, are deemed 'bucketheads'. It involves pulling an empty two-litre cola bottle slowly out of a bucket of water, while cooking up pot on a piece of minutely punctured foil gripped to the bottleneck. The smoke is drawn into the bottle, the foil removed, and the designated buckethead quickly exhales, puts their lips to the opening and inhales the entire contents of the bottle. It is the most efficient way to smoke pot, but apparently not widely done (although everyone I know has tried it). It seems my brain is making a lot of brackets . . . and at the moment, making up my brain is about three buckets . . . But let me rewind my meandering musings and set the scene.

Ash, Daisy, Jamie, Danny, Trixie, Limbo and three goths

I don't know are sat round this bucket in Ash's flat in the centre of town, as if the bucket was a campfire and we were scouts making smores. Jamie I've known since we were in nappies, and Danny, Limbo and Ash come from Osford, so we all grew up playing together out on the waste, a stretch of woodland-cum-rubbish-dump, where we made our dens out of old washing machines and chicken wire, and now here we are together, again, still, giggling in a dark, dank den of a living room. It's sick and it's reassuring and it's sad and it's pathetic how life repeats itself. We haven't changed since we were eight, but as reality emerges before us, hope fades away, and we search for greater highs and deeper lows to escape boredom and deny our inevitable acquiescence to the monotony of life. That's the pot turning me into Socrates, or similar. Who am I kidding? I'm disgusting. I giggle and choke on it, a bitter lump in my throat. I squeeze up my face tight, and stay dead still.

Ash sleepily lets smoke expel from her mouth. I catch her cherry-flavoured lip gloss on the air. 'What's wrong with you?'

'Nothing.' I relax my face. 'Nothing.'

An hour later the guys, including myself, leave in better spirits to a wicked night out. Ash and the girls stay behind to wait for Ella, Josh and a lass called Sally that I once got off with. To my shame she is now fat, and a chav.

4

What Kind of Fucking Stupid Name Is Rainbow?

'WHAT kind of FUCKING STUPID name is Rainbow?' The club is packed and it's 3am before we spill out onto the promenade. As usual I'm holding forth in the spotlight, the others blinded by my winning combination of sex appeal, humour and overbearing cockiness (because I'm now twatted). There's the shouting of drunk lasses, there's fighting skinheads and there's the sea less than fifty yards away, the waves crashing over each other wildly as if in a rush to join in with the party and compete with the noise. All the while Will Flicker, known as Flick, acts the jester, and tonight he's on fucking top form, the King of Scorn, all the lesser mortals crowding around him admiringly to laugh at his witty comments and cheap jibes. What a cock.

'Yeah!' Ella chimes in, acting blonde (not a big stretch for Ella). 'Imagine saying, "Hi, I'm *Rainbow*."'

'Let me take you to my pot of gold,' I make another blinding crack. 'I bet her boyfriend's a leprechaun.' Mike snorts alcopops out of his nose and I nudge him and whisper loudly, 'The height makes him perfect for easy-access muff-diving.'

'Bahahahaha,' Jamie chokes on his cigarette smoke. 'And his ginger beard tickles in a really good way on my woohoo!'

Ella giggles. 'And his little green clothes make him really easy to coordinate with.'

Back to me 'for something funnier but more obscene' (and I actually say that out loud): 'I only appear if it's very . . . WET . . . indeed.' Oh yes, every daft prick there laughs, much louder than they did for Jamie or Ella. Too easy. I'm too good, that's why.

A voice from behind me adds to our banter. 'Yeah, she must be a right whore!'

'All right! Calm down, that's taking it too far.' I turn and find myself right in the face of a girl about my age, one of the late-night slags probably, but there's a fullness to her lips and a light in her eyes, which I think are gently mocking me although I'm not sure yet why, implying better health. Her hair is scruffy, a dark frieze about her face, her makeup light and her complexion pale, not orange like Ash and the others. 'Who are you then? You out with Ashley?' I say, expecting a quick answer, gearing myself up for a bit of banter.

'You first.' Her directness blindsides me. The right corner of her mouth grins, daringly, proudly. I stop moving with my Beck's halfway to my mouth. Cheeky bitch. Sexy too. I almost blush but manage to wait for about three seconds then give her an 'oh-you-want-to-play-games' look (slightly suggestive, with a backwards movement of the head, followed by a slight nod forward – damn smooth). I then cock my head in a substitute shrug, say 'Will Flicker,' pause, 'but everyone calls me Flick,' then grin and take a swig. Champion.

I'm feeling on top of the world, cock of the walk and somewhere in the reaches of my mind I hear a lone sober thought quietly wonder if I could be very, very drunk. Not just superficially and amusingly drunk, but deeply, and importantly, drunk. But the thought is fleeting. I continue.

'And you?' I shoot her a questioning, Brad-Pitt-from-*Fight-Club*-I'm-so-hot look. The thought becomes a disdainful voice: 'maybe you should calm down'. I ignore it, focused instead on what I've now realised is a very attractive lass, who my whisky-sodden and stoned brain believes without doubt will be getting off with me under the pier by closing time. Oh yes. Her smile stretches, her full ripe lips part like a tantalising femme fatale and involuntarily I imagine them on the tip of my dick. She grins showing her teeth.

'My name . . .'

'Yes, baby?' Baby. Chuh. I'm pulling out all the stops.

'Is Rainbow.'

The voice from the back of my mind slams into my frontal lobe, deadpan, and loud in my ear: 'TIT'.

5

The Morning After

I wake up wishing I wasn't waking up. It's light and someone in the house has got the radio on loud, playing that song
about getting all the girls. Tommo, my brother, older and
wiser and yet somehow with much poorer taste in music,
must be over for his regular Saturday morning visit. It's
something he's done for a few years now, since he and Nikki
moved into their own place, and I think it's somehow tied
in to his image of being a 'real man', coming round to give
his wee shortie mam a hug and slap Dad matily on the back,
then drink beer and cook a fry-up. It's like one day he was a
normal teenager, then the next he became this responsible,
I-don't-ever-cry, talk-in-monosyllables 'bloke' and now I
can only ever have a conversation with him about football
or doing up his house. Don't get me wrong, it's nice, but
there's only so much leaning against the kitchen counter and
sighing I can do before I get bored, lose concentration and
fall over.

Still, it's nice that he cares. It'd be great if he waited 'til
at least midday to care though, fuck the early morning. I
groan. I try to drift off but it's too loud, so I shout from my
mattress on the floor (I feng shui-d my six-foot-short child's
bed out to the garbage last year, when the headboard started
to give me neck-ache).

'Shut the fuck up!' No one replies and the music continues. I'm indignant. How dare he? Twat. I bet he's doing it on

purpose to get me up. It's fucking Saturday and it's only . . . I'm squinting at the clock . . . eleven thirty.

'Ohhhhhhhhh.'

My brain shuts off for another half hour and the next thing I'm aware of is being rock hard. I roll over onto my back and start pulling at my dick. I'm still fairly unconscious at this point and last night just hasn't entered my head yet. As far as I know, I went back to Ash's, listened to her cry, pissed the night away and walked home like every Friday, but as I wank, images start appearing in my mind. Parted red lips, tits peering from a ruffled top, darkly suggestive eyes, soft chocolate-coloured hair flicking into my face, and as I come I remember: 'Rainbow-oh-*oh-OHHHHH*'.

A few seconds pass in which I realise the radio is now off. I hear footsteps on the stairs and suddenly my door flies open and Tommo enters, deadpan as ever. 'Oi, Will – our Nikki's made baguettes, so come down and get one if you want. Nice wang.' He turns to go.

I pull my duvet cover over myself. 'Thanks, Tommo.'

6

Questions

Monday comes and I kick through the school gates as the bell for registration stops ringing. Our year has 120 people in it, and we're split into four forms. My form room is at the top of a stone staircase, past the library and the radiators, where a Year Eight who fancies me waits every morning for an eye-fuck. Today I wink at her and she smiles, picks up her bag and skips happily away down the stairs, presumably to her own form's registration. I must make her constantly late. Luckily Dr Stiles, or Timothy as I like to call him, doesn't give a shit if I'm late or not, so I walk in to the sound of him mumbling my name in the register, clap him on the shoulder and shout 'here' in a confident, suave, twatty way. I then sit casually on a desk in the front row, where the rest of the gang instantly lean in asking me about Rainbow and drown out names beginning M to W (there are no names that start X, Y or Z).

My group of mates is ten strong, or at least we always refer to ourselves as 'the ten of us' even when we count nine or eleven, and most of us are in my form, 11S (S for Stiles). I chose to sit us on the front row because at the time it seemed hysterically ironic, now it's just habit. I think you get away with more on the front row. Keep your enemies close, I say. So we sit, me on the desk, Jamie on his chair next to me, Mike knelt on his, Ash and Daisy further along the row both sucking Chupa Chups, and Ella sat on her boyfriend

Josh's lap behind them, everybody leaning in to hear what I have to say.

It's a tough call to say who is the second funniest in the group after myself, but points for being in equal parts inventive and crude as fuck go to Jamie, who once wrote his own theme tune, titled 'Deepthroatin' Jimbo', and sang it so often that a form two years below us learnt the whole thing, and then was kept in over lunch for busting out the second verse, which is all about necrophilia, during a History lesson. Despite what some people might think about this, girls actually love it. He regularly texts me to let me know he can't hang out because he's 'up to his neck in snatch'.

Ash does have her moments, though Mike is Jamie's main contender, having one of those senses of humour where you just don't think the person is going to be funny until they come out with a blinder. Mike looks too shy and too ginger to be hot shit in the laughs department, but he's a loyal and trustworthy mate who will quietly slip in something so hilarious you actually pee a little bit. 'Spotting humour' we call it, although if it's really epic, Jamie refers to it as 'skidmark humour'. Mike and me have been growing apart lately though. He doesn't really do drugs. He doesn't protest or anything gay like that. He just doesn't show up when we make a plan to smoke up, which is always awkward the next day, like I know I'm being avoided but I'm not sure how to feel about it because I kind of agree with him that me doing them is genuinely fucking stupid.

Ella and Daisy are too dumb to be hilarious. Josh made the mistake of getting a steady girlfriend in school when nobody else has one. Now he has to be on his best behaviour when Ella's around and then when she's not, he tries too hard and it's embarrassing for all of us who witness it.

My other mates, who really only have guest spots in the

group, aren't in our form. They include Dildo, who is two years older than us and repeating his GCSEs in another form in our year, Danny, who is eighteen and a brickie and a good mate of Dildo's, and Trixie and Limbo who used to go here but left last year and are now townies, i.e., they hang around in town.

Trixie lives with her thirty-year-old boyfriend in a council flat in the centre of Langrick. It's a bit of a weird, sad relationship, in that she's suddenly started taking E and talking about babies, and her boyfriend is clearly an unemployed wanker who can't find anyone his own age to go out with. He rings her up when she's hanging out with us to call her a cheating cunt and then talks about getting married the rest of the time. She used to go out with Limbo, but her boyfriend made her delete his number. Limbo still lives with his parents on one of the Osford estates, but spends most of his time in Sandford city on the graze for fresh grass, if you catch my drift.

And then there are the people who aren't in our gang, but are the supporting characters, shall we say, and since the Langrick-Osford-Ness area isn't huge and pretty much everyone who lives here grew up here, we all have the same supporting characters in our lives. These include the slightly older role models like Tommo and Nikki and Gav and Tee, although the latter two are reverse-role models, in that they serve as cautionary tales for the rest of us. Then there are the 'destructive' supporting characters: the petty drug dealers like the lovable-but-fucked Kyle Craig, a raging film buff with a GSOH and a death wish; the drunks who buy alcohol for us under-aged folk; the small-town pimps who would never think of themselves as pimps but sort of ended up doing a favour for a female friend who needed some cash, where they asked their mates if any of them were horny.

Those sort of supporting characters are mild scum, but not the worst. The worst are the villains of the piece, people like Fez, who you just don't want to mess with. They've been in prison and had enough raps on their knuckles to make them bleed. It's just been for odd bits and bobs so far but you know something serious is just around the corner. They always get questioned by the police, when stuff goes missing, or when people get knifed to death down near the railway line, because they hang out there and because everybody knows if they didn't have a hand in it, they sure as shit turned a blind eye.

Ash kicks the table to get my attention and I stop gazing out the window and raise an eyebrow at her suggestively, in default Flick-and-Ashley mode.

'So what happened with the lesbian?' Ash, clearly jealous, raises pencil-thin eyebrows at me.

'She muff-dived me,' I grin back.

'She fucking didn't!' says Daisy, shocked. Me and Mike exchange a look and Mike bursts out laughing.

'I'd muff-dive her,' chimes in Jamie. 'I saw her at Langrick market, Sunday, she was well fit.'

'Muff-diving is oral, right?' Daisy asks, high-pitched and confused.

'What was she doing at Langrick market?' Me to Jamie.

Mike to Daisy: 'Yeah, a muff is a minge.'

Jamie to me: 'I dunno. Buying shit.'

'What does she look like?' Josh, leaning around Ella.

Ella, pulling Josh back: 'What do you care?'

Josh to Ella: 'Fucking hell, woman.'

Me, faux-coughing: 'Pussy-whipped.'

'Did anything happen?' Mike to me.

'It will.' Me, grinning cockily, to Mike.

Mike, laughing, then deadpan, to me: 'Hey, Will . . . you're a cock.'

'Yes,' I say proudly. 'Yes I am.' We crack up.

'So is she a lesbian?' Ash demands loudly, clearly not enjoying the lack of attention.

'No, she's not a lesbian,' I say smugly.

'Did you get her number?'

'No, because unlike some people I'm not a manwhore.'

'Um, incorrect use of the term manwhore, don't you think?'

I shake my head.

'Since I'd have to be a *man* . . .'

I nod my head.

'. . . to be a manwh— oh, I see. Ha ha. Ash is a man. You're so fucking funny, Will Flicker, what a sophisticated sense of humour.' Ash spits her lollipop stick at me and it stays on my tie. 'So basically you didn't get anywhere with her then.' The bell rings again and she and Daisy jump off the table and adjust their Wonderbras.

'My dearest Ashley,' I say, as we gather up our bags and get ready to leave for first period. 'I shall have you know that the young woman in question eye-fucked me so sincerely and so intimately that I felt at once very turned on, all of a flutter in my heart, violated – but in a good way – and that she was most definitely, definitively, *not* a lesbian.'

The gang laugh and Ash rolls her eyes at me as the guys and girls make an even split and we head down the stairs and off to Biology.

'*All of a flutter in my heart?*' Jamie repeats, shaking his head disapprovingly at me. 'Homo.'

I grin and think of Rainbow, as I've been doing dreamily all weekend, perhaps with little information on which to base my feelings, but sincerely all the same. I decided on Sunday, somewhere between the leg of lamb and the sherry trifle at Tommo and Nikki's house, that I really, really liked her, and not in your basic 'wahay, she's fit' way – which for me, picky as I am, isn't enough to get me to like anyone. There has to be chemistry and she has to have charm and brains and beauty and, in general thus far, be a figment of my imagination and completely unattainable. Fucking Disney. Back to Rainbow. Yes, I'll admit, at the moment we met I was pretty far gone, but I'm certain it wasn't just alcohol that had made her so unbelievably sexy. And surprisingly, it wasn't her face or body either. I couldn't get over her eyes. With the lack of light they'd looked black, but I'd felt something in them, like an electricity, like they were wider than everyone else's. I describe things fucking shit sometimes. I always think it's the hard nuts that get gooiest over girls though . . . at least, that's how I'll explain it if questioned. Not that I'm a particularly hard nut. Anyway. Where was I? It was basically like Rainbow was more alive than the rest of them. She was clearly switched on in ways we didn't get in Clyde County, clearly intelligent, clearly a challenge, and now that I'd come down from my drug-fuelled high, I figured there was very little chance she'd want to talk to me. Although I knew I was smart I was flunking my GCSEs, I was pretty spotty from smoking and although I was witty and could entertain my mates I never had anything really interesting to say. I'd thought about stuff. Sometimes I thought about studying politics and cutting out the bullshit and standing up for the underdog – yeah! Girl power! Etcetera. But I didn't know anything about it. Dad tends to tell me I'm thick, which I hate, then talk for hours without saying anything so I never ask him owt, and Mam's a bit vague about legal stuff that isn't to do with *NCIS* and various other telly shows about crime scene investigation.

So I knew I didn't have a ghost of a chance with Rainbow, but I wanted to know about her. Curiosity, I guess. What do you get if you mix those eyes with those lips? What is a girl called Rainbow going to be like? Will she like me: a virgin, a twat and a stoner? Ah, fuck it. I've got to stop being such a dick.

7

The Art of the Right Amount of Stoned

In the meantime I've also got to wait. I don't see this gorgeous switched-on lass around school and, from what I can gather, she might be older than me, so I take a guess that she's at the sixth form college in Ness-on-Sea and that I'll see her out on Friday or Saturday. So I start using a new kind of facewash in preparation for the weekend (you can never say I don't put in the effort) and get on with watching the days waste away again. It doesn't take that long. I spend most of it just stoned enough for days to blur into each other but not stoned enough for Mam and Dad to notice (the perfect amount). I was about to dive into a description of the next few days but let's linger on that thought a little, because of course nothing worth noting is going to happen, and talk about the wonderful life-saving concept of the Right Amount of Stoned.

The right amount of stoned defies physics. The right amount of stoned allows you to be in two places at the same time. The true genius of it is that it makes paying attention whether in class or at home feel like zoning out. And the majority of stoners don't know about it. They are fools, they giggle too much and get away with too little. It's like the quiet rebellion of the A-grade student who is such a genius that actually they need to do no work to get the As. You know them. You're probably jealous of them and bitch a little bit, maybe start a rumour that they're gay or lost their virginity in a car or something. Ash did. Anyway. The student that consistently gets As can rebel as much as they like. They can be rude, they can swear, they can flip a teacher off (and they have the time to do all these things because they did their work in the first five minutes of a fifty-minute lesson), but because they get straight As they can never be expelled. It looks too harsh, particularly because they come to school to be educated and according to the laws of the curriculum they are great at it. They called your mum a cunt, but they are, technically, the best student in your class. A tricky situation for a teacher. For the stoner who perfects the perfect amount of stoned, the situation is the same. When they ask you questions, you can answer. Your work may be shite, but it is done. Hence, the punishment can never be so severe. If you are doped up to your eyeballs, however, they can spot you and turf you out faster than you can slur, 'No I'm not stoned, errr, it's . . . it's . . . I've had a stroke!' (true story).

Last summer I was not into drugs. In any way. I thought they were Bad News. Ash had started hitting the bong by then, thanks to various older sexual friends, but Mike and me spent most of our time playing video games, swapping music, surfing and not going out with girls we liked. In the innocent light of youth, we were healthy, idealistic idiots, and we thought we were right, and that Ash and Jamie, who had by the end of the summer succumbed to Ash's peer-pressuring and become a stoner, were twats.

But there is something about going back to school, that anyone who has ever been to school can relate to, that gets you down. And I mean so far down you feel like you won't be able to come up. So we go back in the September, and the first week is okay, because there's not that much work and yes you have five deadlines for massive holiday projects but you did them in detention in the summer term anyway, so you hand them in and get a new coat and generally piss about. Play football at lunch. I don't do that much any more either. Then it gets to October and there's that nice frosty feeling on your nose and you hang out at the park and the girls you get off with round the back of the town hall taste of chips and hot chocolate and that's all good too. But then the days start to drag and when you wake up in the morning it's so fucking cold. And you start to have to hand in work you haven't done. You have fifteen different classes and they each give you 'just half hour a week', and excuse me for being sarcastic, but it all adds up. People start turning sixteen and your birthday is in August, so it doesn't happen for you, which makes you a baby. And still unable to buy smokes. Your fingers cramp up and you actually hurt from the cold when you go outside at lunch and break, but you have to, unless you hide in the toilets or the woodwork room or hang about a radiator intimidating people away, because them's the rules, kids! But then of course you hang about those radiators and tell prefects to knob off and you get lunchtime dits (detentions), which is actually a plus because it means you're in a warm classroom while everyone else freezes their knacks off on the field. And then comes the advantage of knowing the Right Amount.

January arrives and you realise you have nothing to look forward to. Even Easter is balls, because this is England, so it's still fucking cold and all you get at Easter is chocolate, which you can shake out of the vending machine next to the Maths block anyway. So you end up getting drunk in the lunch hour to pass the time. Then you go behind the pavilion, which is a little hut at the end of the field, and you meet Dildo, who is a friend of yours, and he's sitting with Andrew Bell, who isn't a friend of yours, but appears amicable enough as he passes you his spliff and makes a space for you on the grass next to him. You take a drag. You shrug. There isn't much to this. You're there for ten minutes, in which time you smoke about half a joint on your own. You start to giggle. You think, oh I get it, so you reach for another drag.

But then Andrew's hand stops you.

'No, mate.' Your eyes meet, like lovers. 'No.' And he pulls your ear to his lips, and he lets you in on the secret, on the Art of the Right Amount of Stoned.

8

God's Punchline

The only remotely interesting thing that happens before my next Rainbow encounter is that I have to go see my academic tutor at school, which is worrying since I haven't really been seeing many of my teachers of late. Ms Casper is, I'd say, late thirties and not great looking for it, and we don't get on well, because the first time I met her I played my usual flirty charm and she accused me of misogyny and mild sexual harassment (I had to look up the first one after the session but I got the point – she's not a fan). Today I was scheduled for a meeting at 2pm so when I wandered in at 2.15 with the faint nicotine-y scent on my breath only slightly subdued by four hastily crunched mints, I was prepared for a bollocking. 'Miss Casper?'

'It's MS!' A shout springs from the corner of the room, but I can't see her and for a moment my brain thinks, oh my god, she's dead and this is her ghost. But then no, in reality that would never happen. I imagine my mind glaring at itself. Bell end.

'What?'

I realise too late I've said bell end, out loud, and to the teacher's arse, as she sits with her back to me, crouched behind her desk. 'Oh, sorry, nothing, Ms Casper. Can I help?'

'I don't think so. It's the computer. I'm trying to get it to reboot so we can do your application for college.'

I bend down to see the wiring. Nothing seems out of place but there is a reboot button and I shove my chewed pencil into it. The screen starts beeping and I press return. Hey presto, computer rebooted. I can't believe this woman is a) employed and b) computer illiterate. They should have replaced the teachers when they replaced the system, is my thinking. I type in the codes and password cockily and whack the computer with my forefinger.

'It's the Flick that does it.' Yeah, look at that double entendre. I'm so smart and hot.

'Right.' Ms Casper's bespectacled head pops up from behind the table and she pats her hair and brushes the crumbs off her cardigan. I look about the desk. Hobnobs. I take one and offer her the packet. 'No thank y— Will, give me those! Sit down!'

I pull up a chair next to her.

'Now, we still haven't decided what subjects you're applying for. We've got you down for Ness Sixth Form College?'

'Yeah, for law.'

'Right.' She blows her nose loudly. I move my chair back. 'Do you want to be a lawyer?'

Was that a hint of sarcasm I detected? I frown.

'I'm not being sarcastic, Mr Flicker, I believe that's your territory. I'm simply asking what you want to do so we get you the right A Levels.'

- 'Politics.'

'Okay . . .' She stares at the screen for what seems like forever, licks her lips cautiously and presses return.

'D'you want me to do that?'

'No, no, that's okay . . . This is what school is about . . . learning . . .'

'Miss—'

'Ms. Now, Will, your report card from last term wasn't

very . . . good. You know you'll have to work hard to get high enough GCSE grades to actually get into college? And then when you get there . . . it's not like here – you can't just swan in and out of lessons when you like, they're very strict.'

'What? I don't just—'

'Oh, Flick – sorry, Will – please don't, for the want of a better word, bullshit me, I'm not an idiot, even if I don't appear to be exactly computer-literate . . . they really should have replaced us with the system, or at least given us training . . . but I know you're smart and you can do better than you do but then you don't, do you? I'm just wondering if college is the right option for you . . . but there's really no alternative. If you want to go to university, you have to do A Level examinations at college and for someone as bright as you an apprenticeship is a waste of brains. You certainly don't want to end up at the steel works—'

'Hey, hold on, my brother works at the works,' I object, even though I've just discovered new respect for *Ms* Casper. So many of my teachers think I'm thick and it pisses me off but it does mean I can get away with doing badly and not be hassled about it. They can't be fucked with you, unless you're the child of a fellow teacher in which case they have to be or they get complaints. I used to be in Maths and English sets all on my own in primary school, when I was a little kid, 'cause I was so far ahead of the other kids but do any of the teachers here know that? Hell no. So it's nice to think Ms Casper is aware that I'm smart, even if it does now mean she expects things of me. But I can't have her undermining a family member. Even the best of the staff never understand about life here. They all come from universities in Lancaster or London and they're doing their bit for poor people before sodding off to better places. I flip into defender-of-the-people mode. 'What's wrong with the works, it's a good, honest job! Half the people are on the dole round here. If you're at the works you're earning a living for your family and working hard for it!'

I suddenly realise I'm actually defending a position I'd previously only scorned . . . out of what? Pride? Panic? Could I really end up there? I'm starting to get depressed. The problem with getting qualifications here is that you have to move away to use them. Another catch-22, since you're supposed to be working to earn the money for your mam and dad to retire on, and you have to move away, and then never see them, to do it. And Mam'd miss me. It's hard in a family of men, and what with Tommo gone all manly and monosyllabic now. I'm the only one who'll chat with her about her interests and what she did that day and how Brenda up in Ness has a new flat and is fretting about whether to have chintz curtains or not (NO, Brenda, NO).

'When am I ever going to get the chance to be a politician in Clyde County?' I mutter. 'We only have one, and I bet they have a degree . . . and that's another fucking three years . . .' I trail off darkly.

We sit in silence for a minute while she stares at the computer and I pick the skin from around my fingernails.

'Oh, fuck it.' She gives up on the computer. 'The thing is, Flick, life wasn't meant to be perfect. Perfect is a concept human beings have created because we are intrinsically afraid. And fear is justifiable but you can't let it get in the way of living your life. You can't think, "Well, trying takes courage and it's easier to be lazy, so I'll just sit on my bum all day" because you end up with nothing, and I mean absolutely nothing. There are people I went to school with who attended the very best universities and when they got out they expected the world to be their oyster and it wasn't, so they went back home, sulked about it and they still work at Tesco's. Eight years after we graduated – don't jump in shock, I know I look forty, thank you . . . at least I'm doing what I wanted to do. Everything that's worth anything takes effort Flick. You have to decide what you want to do from an early age and go for it full speed to get it. Otherwise you end up with jack all.' She pauses and looks straight at me. 'If you go the way you're going Flick, you'll be the most articulate person to ever have failed his GCSEs. Now go on, have a think about it and come see me next Monday. I'll be in here all day, for my sins.'

She dives back in to the mass of wires behind the monitor as I leave the room reeling. Picture this. Fifteen years old and you have to decide what you want to do for the rest of your life, or you basically don't get one. God's punchline: 'All right I'll give you the gift of life, but you better make up your mind about it quickly or it's eighty years of sweet FA!' I imagine all of mankind lining up in front of an angel and being presented with this conundrum. I imagine the clock from *Countdown*, the hand giving me thirty seconds to decide the rest of my life and then boo-doop-boo-doop-boo-doop-doo-doop bow! Sorry, times up, no go. How the frig am I supposed to decide now? And if I do decide on one thing then choose another in a couple of years, haven't I just wasted my time?

As I kick my way through the door into Biology another thought crosses my mind – did I just find Ms Casper, in her own people power rant, that little bit sexy? Well . . . I said I liked intelligent women. Oh, Jesus. Maybe that's god's punchline.

9

Homelife

Before I know it, the weekend draws near and I start to feel apprehensive, and maybe a little bit excitable. I'm sitting with my mam and dad in the living room, which is warm and cosy, with the coal fire on and the smell of Domestos coming from the doorway to the kitchen. That last bit was sarcasm. Learn to love it.

I'm flicking through the channels when I hear a mention of Clyde County and pause, watching the newsreader. 'Sandford's been voted the worst place to live in England,' I say, turning the volume up on *Look North*.

'Oh, right,' says Dad, not looking up. He rustles his newspaper.

'Yeah . . . *officially*.' It's Thursday night and we're in front of the telly with Jack and Coke, and Mam, nibbling animal-like at the corners of her chicken kiev and micro-chips. She's way too skinny is our mam. Races around all the time working in the supermarket and in her other job as a cleaner and helping out at the nursery with the local kids and never eats anything but wine and leftovers. I continue, trying to wind Dad up. 'We were sixth last year. We've climbed the ranks!' Silence. Mam licks her lips and picks up her Pinot Grigio. 'Car crime capital of England . . .' The reporter frowns at his notes in the clean symmetry of the grey studio. 'They haven't even bothered to come and do the report here.'

'Well, son, that's probably because they're worried they're

going to get their car nicked!' Dad laughs at his own wittiness.

'Yeah, by the likes of you,' says Mam, accusingly through a chip (I'll never use that phrase again).

'Oh! Well, thanks for the vote of confidence, Mam! Go on, that's right! Giggle at me, you drunken floozy!' She smiles into her plate and protests when I plant a big greasy kiss on her left cheek.

'Get off! Watch the telly!'

'I am.' I catch a line of the report. 'D'you hear that, Dad?' I say, glancing at him slyly. 'We're number one for domestic violence.'

Dad slams his paper onto the table beside him and, shouting, walks across the room towards me and spits into my face. 'Oh, and I suppose that's my fault, is it?!'

He spins round, walks into the kitchen and we hear him fumbling for another JD and Coke. He opens the door with a resounding crack as it hits the coffee table beside it. 'Get up those fucking stairs right now!' He looms up over me, so close I can smell his whisky breath.

'Me? What have I done?'

'Answering back, that's what!'

'No, I'm not going! You go if you're that bothered!' I turn my head back to the telly.

'Don't backchat me, son, this is my bloody house!'

'Oh, yeah,' I smirk, knowing full well Tommo has covered all the mortgage payments since Dad got laid off. 'So you pay the bills do you?'

'FUCKing little shit.' He lunges at me, clawing at my shoulder and pulls me off my armchair and up to his height. My plate flies to the floor. I roll my arm over to throw off his grip, push his hand away and take a pace back.

'Don't you fucking dare, Dad. I swear to god. Don't you

fucking dare.' We stand erect, facing each other, head tilted down like bulls ready to charge and I realise, unsettlingly, that I look like him. I shake my head. 'I'm going upstairs. Are you all right, Mam?'

'Yeah, I'm fine, love.'

I would pause for a second with disbelief but this is all routine in our house, so I roll my eyes at her with disgust and she doesn't catch me, and wouldn't understand why. It always seems to me that feminism never got this far up north. All these women sitting at home, ignoring their husbands who shout and paw and beat them down until they resemble mice, squeaking quietly, hovering uncertainly in their figure-drenching clothes. These are our mothers and we love and hate them. They are of an age, a place, a time and a type that is recognisable to us, their children, by sight and for acquiescing to this, I don't think we, I don't think I, will ever forgive her. I scoop my food back onto my plate and jog upstairs, slump on my shabby mattress and eat the rest of my cold chips in silence, attempting half-heartedly to conjure up images of Rainbow, tomorrow, Ash's arse, surfing, the pot I've got in my underwear drawer – trying to think of something more positive than patricide, holding onto my hopes for Friday night.

IO

The Weekend Cometh (and So Do I?)

Friday arrives with a bang, a bong, and a bottle of White Lighting. Fucking classy. By ten we're in Ritzies, the etiquette being not to arrive early as it is unfashionable, still light, and because getting smashed in the bar is more expensive than buying a twelve pack of Carling and going round Ash's beforehand. So, Ritzies, as far as Langrick is concerned: the nightclub of nightclubs. Sweat (and a bit of vomit) on the floor, the walls, the floor-to-ceiling mirrors, the underage clientele and the forty-something Tesco-worker mildly retarded paedos who supply Ash with free-flowing alcopops, but when the night matures and the gang is all here, the stars align, and as promised, it is a wicked night. Dildo and Danny, both eighteen, flash their IDs at the door and we flood in behind them, waving Blockbusters membership cards drunkenly at the doormen. Ash and Daisy are lezzing up by the bar to get themselves free Bacardi Breezers, Josh, Mike and Jamie bag us a corner booth, and familiar faces greet me warmly as I do a recce about the dance floor. The lights are low, I'm smashed enough to be confident but not enough to be a cock and la pièce de résistance (although if she asked me I don't know why I'd be résisting), I clock Rainbow over the other side of the dance floor, in a stripy rainbow dress and red platforms, her hair spiked out about her face (reminding me simultaneously of Marla from *Fight Club*, Sonic the Hedgehog and a dandelion clock), and a spidery black cardigan clinging to her arms.

'Aw,' I think, temporarily forgetting to be cool. 'She looks cute.'

Sharam's 'Party All the Time' is playing, and I swagger over to the DJ who happens to be a mate of mine on account of the fact that Tommo occasionally works on the door as a bouncer, and he shouts to me in greeting. 'All right, knobend?'

'All right, Gordy?' (Gordy the Geordie.) 'How do?'

'Good thanks, man! Had your sister in 'ere t'other night though, wanted to ask you about her.'

'Oh ay, Teagan?'

'Yeah, she living with someone new now?'

'I don't know, she never comes round. Tommo drives to see her sometimes but, well, you know. It's not that they don't get along, but they're into different things.' This is quite a lot to shout at Gordy, and he can't lip-read as I'm facing away from him, staring at Rainbow. He taps me on the shoulder with a vinyl to get my attention, shakes his head and points to his ears.

'Anyway,' I watch him mouth. 'Has she got another one on the way?'

I cup my hand round my ear, too absorbed with the presence of Rainbow to have listened properly. 'Yer what?'

'She looked pregnant.'

'Oh . . .' There is a pause while I digest this information, although with the music and the neon club lights my instantaneous nausea probably isn't that distinguishable. 'Are you sure it wasn't just kebab fat?'

'No man, it was only her stomach. She looked pretty far gone. You're gonna be an uncle! Sort of.' He grins as I pull a face.

'Oh, ah-way man!' I put down my drink, put on a brave face, shrug gamely and then darkly think, I hope she's not too far gone to get an abortion. Which is a bit of a sick wish. I glance out across the club and decide to ignore this little bit of info for the night, and put all my efforts into befriending and then, hopefully, charming Rainbow. 'Gordy, can you put on a bit of Fedde Le Grand for us?'

Gordy spins 'Put Your Hands Up for Detroit'. I pinpoint Rainbow across the other side of the room. She is watching me. I look over at Ash, and she makes a 'V' with her fingers and licks it. Jamie and Mike give me the thumbs up and start humping the table. I shake my head, frown at them and look back at Rainbow. She is watching my mates, then looks back at me and laughs. I start walking towards her, feeling hot and suddenly nervous. My heart is racing, I'm sweaty-palmed, excited. Last time I felt this way I was four and Katie Barker picked me to be her husband in a game of 'Will you marry me?' I had her on my lap the whole lunch-time and I sweated so much I dehydrated and got sunstroke. Fuck, my brain thinks, stop getting distracted . . . you could step in vomit.

Rainbow winds her way through the dancers towards me, never breaking eye contact. Then suddenly, I step down onto the lowest level of the floor, wind through a group of chavtastic girls, who pop gum and grab my bum, and when I appear again, she is gone. I stand frozen, confused, waiting for her. I feel a tap on my left shoulder. I look over it, but she is on my right.

'Gotcha,' she grins, bright white teeth flash between scarlet lips. I'm caught off guard and I turn into her, bumping her on the shoulder. Rainbow laughs. 'Wanna dance?' she says cheekily.

'In a minute,' I murmur, shyly, mesmerised by her beauty.

I smile and, looking for a way to get back control, I say, 'I wanna kiss you first.'

She smiles her pouty little smile, leans in with her full lips parted and then pulls suddenly backwards, her perfume left hanging in the air around me, and smiles widely, her tooth catching her lip. 'Not yet, but nice try.' And she is away and onto the floor. She dances alone, hips swaying, breasts silhouetted in the half-light, her eyes closed and I watch her for a minute before wondering what the fuck I'm doing standing there like a prick, and go to join her. My friends and her friends make a little group about us, though mostly Mike and Jamie just jump up and down to the beat, ask me when I'm going to Dildo's, and tell me the girl I'm dancing with is hot, loudly, on purpose, and all within ear-shot of Rainbow. She laughs gamely, and leans in, I think to whisper to me, but then her mouth is on mine, her tongue licks my tongue, and we're pressed against each other, getting off hornily in the middle of the floor.

II

Snatched Facts

I notice a lot about Rainbow that night. When I think back to it, I noticed more about Rainbow in those first few brief, snatched meetings than I did even in the following few weeks. I've wondered since if it was like that for everyone. I remember how she seemed so forward and honest, but at the same time reserved and private. Maybe it was that she was honest with me and reserved with everyone else. I noticed how she always drank with a straw, took lime in every drink, I watched the way she walked, a slow, sexy wiggle when she was relaxed and then, if walking to get to somewhere, the same long movement but sped up. She always looked like she had long legs, but she was only five foot three, and her body always seemed to belong to a small woman rather than a large child if you know what I mean. Curvier legs than Ash, real muscles in her calves and thighs, a good bum, a slim waist, not simply malnourished from a diet of mini Mars bars and canteen burgers, I'm talking healthily slim, toned. She had thin wrists and long thin arms, blue eyes, not baby blue like most people, but this dark troubled ocean blue. Her hair and whole aura gave off a hippyish quality. She didn't smoke or drink much, and she was always happy unless she was gripped by mini-depressions, which she had occasionally. She said it was down to hormones and took some herbal stuff for it. She was polite and incredibly well mannered and thought of manners as kindnesses. And she was always asking me about myself. I'd never been with anyone who wanted to know what I wanted to do for a living, if I wanted to travel, what my passions were. What my first kiss was like. That first night after we kissed in the club she made me lay my head on her lap in a corner of the carpeted back room, and asked me if I had any brothers or sisters. I had never had anyone before who thought to ask things like that. She would question me too. The first time she saw me light up she said, 'Hey, you know, I heard something about cigarettes, apparently they're bad for your health.' I smirked to make a joke out of it and she held my gaze, not disapprovingly but sincerely, quietly challenging me to dare to do better, until someone asked us the time and my mates started jumping on me, bailing me out of the conversation.

Rainbow has an ethereal quality, like a pixie standing in the centre of a crowd, winking at me. She winks at me a lot.

12

'When the Sun and the Rain Occur at the Same Time' or 'Pros and Cons of the First Girl'

When the club empties its dubious inhabitants are thrown out onto the pavement like vomit from the double doors and Dildo, the oldest of us and playing the big brother role, herds us all together sheepdog-style down the coast road towards the outskirts of town. The gang is staying the night at his flat, 'cause his parents are away visiting family, and Rainbow walks up the road with us. Ash runs on ahead with Daisy, screaming and twirling each other about, tits falling out of their tank tops, Dildo and Jamie stride behind them, Dildo laughing as Jamie holds court, and Ella and Josh follow, arguing viciously. You can see Ella's spit as she hisses in the lamplight. It's a typical picture perfect moment of our gang and I seek out Danny's gaze and grin wryly at him. He winks back, wacks Mike on the back of the head with the palm of his hand, says, 'Come on, gingertits, let's leave two bloody lovebirds alone,' and they jog off after the others, leaving Rainbow and myself bringing up the rear, side by side.

I do a sort of backwards swing with my arm, touch her hand to ask her a question, 'D'you want a palmo?' and then keep hold of it. Not the suavest of movements, but a brave effort. A palmo, by the way, is basically a local delicacy. Its full name is chicken parmesan, and it comprises of a pizza-base-sized slab of chicken covered in breadcrumbs, with some sort of vegetable sauce thrown on it, then topped with cheese. It looks like lasagne but shitter, though after a night out on the tiles it tastes, I swear, like *heaven*. Apparently someone's dad invented it about forty years ago, though that might be an urban legend. It's our way of life. We work in steel and eat palmos. This is why all Sandford players are crap.

Anyway, back to the matter at hand, the first attempt at hand-holding. When you're first with a girl, everything is a first time. First kiss, first hand-hold, first fuck. These all have to be negotiated, worried about (or so I would assume with the fucking aspect of things, not having been privy to that debacle yet. We'll walk that plank when we come to it. I've given myself an aim of five minutes and from what I've heard that's pushing it). I shake my brain in my head.

You've got to stop thinking about this, says the voice that helps me out when I'm wankered. What if it happens tonight?

Fuck. Now I'm panic stations go. Fuck. Fuck. Fuck. But it won't, will it? Rainbow, as we know, is classy.

Well, the voice murmurs, classy but unpredictable.

Look, I argue back, she is not a simple Langrick bird. Her accent is posher . . . Fuck. I realise with a sudden jolt of marijuana-induced alarm (the type of alarm where a piece of information thus far clouded in pot smoke rises from the fog like an epiphany, only about half an hour too late to be helpful) that I don't even know where she's from. I know she's just moved to Ness, in the house next to Ella, but what about before that? What if someone asks and I can't tell them? Jesus shit Jesus. What if someone asks her last name?!

Flick, chill out, says the voice. As long as we're not getting fucked, nothing can go that horribly wrong.

We turn into Dildo's road.

'This is where his place is,' I hear, coming remarkably calmly from my mouth. 'You want me to walk you home?'

Rainbow turns into Dildo's drive and looks back at me. 'No, I'm okay, thanks,' she smirks. 'I'm coming in.'

I gulp audibly.

'Oh, don't worry,' she says sweetly. 'I'm not going to have sex with you. We'll just do kissing.'

'Oh . . .' I follow her in through the door. 'Okay.'

'Yeah,' she says, skipping up the stairs. 'And other stuff.' She stops, looks back at me, winks and smiles knowingly.

And with that my brain melts in my skull and dribbles out of my ears.

13

Call My Bluff

It is dark. I'm hot and flustered. I can feel my heart beating in my throat. I can smell musky perfume and pizza and cigarettes. I swallow, lean in, my tongue touches another and my lips softly bite another plump lip. I put my hand around a waist that almost fits entirely inside my palm. It is soft and warm. Rainbow, smiling, parts her legs. She takes my right hand gently and slides it up the inside of her thigh, which is milky white and so smooth I shiver and close my eyes for a second. I want to push my face into her thighs and squeeze them. We are in a tiny box room in Dildo's house. It belongs to his eleven-year-old brother, who is away on a sleepover. Beside us is a half-drunk bottle of peach schnapps, the only thing we could raid from Dildo's mum's cupboard, and under the bed is a battered condom I stole from Ash (just in case).

'Will?' I look up through a dark haze at her gorgeous face, honest and bold and sweet and questioning, and I swallow myself back to a higher state of consciousness. She smiles at me and I smile weakly back. I'm so fucking helpless. I want to cry in between her legs. She leans in and slides her tongue into my mouth. I hold her bottom lip, full and delicious, between mine. I've forgotten where my hand is and suddenly I touch something hot, like a pie just out of the oven, but wet too, so I can slide my hand around freely. I let out an 'Oh', and the tip of my middle finger glides easily into her.

It occurs to me for a moment that I might not be very

good at fingering. My last two girlfriends weren't very vocal about anything – I tend to go for shy types – and Sam, who it happened with once on someone's sofa at a party, was gobby about everything: 'FUCK! You're so HOT, Flick', 'My last boyfriend was twenty-five so I'm a fucking MASTER', 'I'm gonna FUCK you like a DOG', 'OH YES, FUCK ME!'

I didn't, and we don't speak any more.

Rainbow slips her tongue into my ear and I'm *back in the room*, like the hypnotist's victims in *Little Britain*, with Rainbow hypnotising me with her eyes. Then suddenly I'm gone again into a different place, where there is no thought, only the moment we exist in, the heat of her pussy and an indescribable tingling in my ear.

'Fuuuuck.'

And I realise that this is it. This isn't reported, I'm not listening to someone else's story. This is my life, me and Rainbow, and at this second I wouldn't trade it for anyone else's. This is exactly where I want to be. I feel more present at this precise moment in time than I have felt for my whole life up until now. Another first. I peel Rainbow off me and hold her face in my hands. She's beautiful. Suddenly shy, I don't say so. Instead I smile and go a bit red, and my vision blurs at the edges. When I pull her towards me, and our lips touch, I sigh a massive breath, part satisfaction, part relief. Soppy twat. I feel like laughing. So I do.

We spend the night together, in the dark, in each other. I only regain a semblance of consciousness at one other point in the night when, with my lips red and swollen from kissing, I shyly and hornily tell her that if she wants anything from me, *anything*, just to ask. She parts her equally swollen lips and with a sweet and so-sexy smile whispers: 'Go down on me, Will.' Holy shit.

PART TWO

I

Space Time Continuum Warp Factor School

In the way that only happens when you're in school and re-peating the same monotonous gobshite routine every day, time runs away from me. It is difficult to understand how one day can seem so ridiculously slow, but months seem to pass where very little worth mentioning occurs. I'm sure in part it is due, in this case, to being young and in love or whatever you'd care to call it, because when you are young the details matter so much and this creates a paradox. On the one hand, as you're watching for every detail you are very much in the moment, time seems to go out the window and all you are left with after the affair is a rosy glow of something sweet, innocent and faintly remembered, a glow in which you happily bask. On the other hand, the tiniest moments can hurt like a knife (like seeing her hold someone else's gaze or break from your own) and become so import-ant, burned on your retina, that it can be unbearable (hence the pot, because we're all so tortured, *sob*).

On a more general note, however, this seemingly simulta-neous speeding up and slowing down of time appears often to come hand in hand with being In School. My hypothesis (since I know you're so interested) is that, in an education system largely based on exam results, there ends up being little to do for the rest of the year. This is also given that if you're smart or have a good teacher you tend to pass the exams, and if you're not, and you don't, you're fucked. Thus they pack the less important eleven months with pointless coursework that, although it does add to our final grade, basically offers no sense of fulfilment as we all know most of the tasks we're set are utter crap, would never happen in the real world and are geared solely towards proving yourself to an instructor and a certain system of grading, and definitively not towards proving to the individual his or her own worth, intelligence or ability. This, my friends, is why every Year Eleven, though in particular the more able, just after receiving their results become puzzled and bewildered over one question. Why is it that during the GCSEs everything is a struggle and you're up 'til 4am every night doing the work (I speak here for the people that actually do it; I'll not shy away from the fact that although I am generally up until 4am, I tend to be mainly wanking and/or watching *Two Pints of Lager and a Packet of Crisps*), then in the exams, which you didn't revise for, you're sat there worried you're missing the point 'cause the supposedly hard questions seem very ABC level, then on results day you get way better grades than you thought you were going to get? Well, hold on to that curve you're graded on because I'm about to give you the Holy Grail of answers to this Mother of questions. It is because (drum roll please) the level of knowledge and intelligence needed to pass a GCSE is very little, but the *amount* of work is mind-shatteringly overwhelming. And so, when people do not pass a GCSE it is not because they are thick (because they would have to be *very* thick to not realise that repeating the Very Simple Textbook Answer to all the Very Simple Textbook Questions asked will get you full marks), but it is because they have not put in the hours to revise for exams/complete all the coursework. Their work is incomplete more often than it is crap, and when it is crap, it is because it took very little time. And thus whether it is laziness, a misunderstanding of this most basic principle of the curriculum, or whether you are just that little bit too stoned to find what you're reading (or what you've written) coherent, the work piles up, you find yourself being chased down corridors by ancient cross-eyed women (Ms White, *who the fuck are you looking at?*) spitting on their cardigans with rage because you haven't handed in a piece of work they *knew* you weren't going to do. They threaten you with suspension because there are only five lunchtime detention slots in the week and you've racked up sixteen and then you find yourself doing more work than you planned on doing, you're working the man hours, your hands are tied and suddenly two weeks of your life are dead and buried and you'll never get your misspent youth back again.

GCSE students, here is my advice: do the coursework, but don't do anything else. When exam time cometh, ask for a copy of the curriculum and revise from that (except for in English, where you will need either to be naturally smart or to make notes). *It will make little difference to your life in the long run. If you want to do anything academic you will need a good degree, so work out which course you want to do, get enough to get on to it, and then put in the work. Or choose one of the many different paths they never tell you about in school. I'm serious. You will never be sixteen again. Throw caution to the wind, cast off the mainsail, do/kiss the girls/boys you always wanted to do/kiss but never did. You know who I mean.*

And I hope you heed that sincerely meant advice.

2

Basking in the After-Gnor

So time flies and I find myself, a fortnight after GNOR (the Glorious Night of Rainbow, hallowed be her name) walking home from the school bus stop through Osford centre, with an old mate of mine, Angie, who now works at our village's one and only pub. Again, she's someone I went to playschool with and we ate dinner together every night for about three years when we were in single digits because our mothers worked in the same supermarket and used to take alternate shifts so they could babysit us. I haven't spoken with Angie since before GNOR, as it shall now formally be known, so I'm happily boring her with every detail of the things she has missed, right down to the composition of Rainbow's irises (very dark blue with a slash of gold through each). I like Angie because she's one of the guys without being too butch and she'll listen to you without trying to get off with you. Plus she always lets me drink for free, even if Rob, the grumpy manager, is watching. She picks at her nose-stud while I struggle to describe the exact curvature of Rainbow's bum.

'So.' Angie flicks dried nose skin to the kerb. 'D'you click with her then?'

'Yeah, I think so. I actually asked her and she said most of the time, clicking takes a while, y'know, you have to get into the other person's rhythm, but she said we fitted instantly, like jigsaw pieces, which I thought was wicked.'

'Completely, I know when I first started seeing Jamie we took a while to click but now when we're together it's awesome—'

'Yeah—' I attempt to butt in. Jamie isn't actually Angie's boyfriend by the way. They have a weird and complicated relationship based on sleeping with each other and being best friends – the downside of being a 'matey' kind of girl. I've had words with Jamie about it, but he says Angie knows the score and if she hasn't got it from the things he's said to her about wanting to sleep about a bit before 'settling' for someone, then she'll probably have got it from watching him sleep about a bit with practically all of our mates. I don't agree with his approach but I have a certain amount of admiration for his big, hairy balls.

'—and there's no awkwardness any more. When we wanna say something we just say it—'

'—yeah, like—'

'It's so simple now.'

Grrr, let me talk about Rainbow, let me talk about Rainbow, let me talk about Rainbow. I'm holding my jaw tight with impatience. She knows I'm not listening so I don't know why she bothers. I bite at my nails. I have to get my sentence out or *I'll die*, thinks my brain.

'Jamie said to me the other week . . . Flick? Are you *shaking*? Oh, for fuck's sake, talk about Rainbow then.'

Ahhhh good. 'Okay, so I said to her did she want a drink and she said . . .' Wicked. I get it all out. By the time we get to our estate I'm still not finished so we sit on the pavement and I talk her ear off for another hour before there's no more to tell and then I go home, eat dinner and have a wank. Bliss.

3

Friends

My time-equals-school-over-disinformation equation proves true, and another pointless couple of weeks go by with little to report. We stay in, go out, shake it all about, drink and shout. Ash shags people and cries, I take a few lines, Daisy gets dumped, we camp in the woods, Mike gets bottled in the face late night near Daisy's place, Ella and Josh fight and make up and fuck loudly next door and I call Ash a whore, always unheard, and we get wankered and Jamie fucks a skank, and I wank and wank and I fail one more test and pass two and flirt my way out of the former and get stoned round the corner. There's flashing lights and later nights and one full moon and nothing new over and over again with no discernible end and all the time, in the back of my mind, I'm seeing colours, lips, tits, hair that flicks, a rainbow of Rainbow.

It's been a fortnight since our first rendezvous and Rainbow is proving as elusive as her namesake. I've got her number and msn off a mutual mate but my casual and, I'd like to think, smooth texts go unanswered, and since I'm reluctant to appear anything but my usual cool and unflappable self I can't beg her for another meet up, but I let it slip that I'm very interested to certain notorious gossips (such as Fat Sal) and I wait for news.

Privately I allow myself to remember her by saying her name. Just once each time, quietly, so as not to jinx it and longingly, because I need, now I know what it means, to feel alive again.

All my friends seem to be ghost versions of themselves. We sit out and smoke up on the field at the back of our school one lunchtime. Gav joins us with a cheery grin, as he sometimes does when there's money to be made on the school field, and starts rolling joints for Josh and telling him about this PCP murder he saw on *Without a Trace*. I can hear him from where we're sat, about ten feet away on a small grassy bank with a good view of the school, saying something about stabbing and laughing like an excited toddler. I suck in the pot and hold it thoughtfully. Dildo starts telling me a story about his sister and I grunt at pauses and think about Rainbow.

'We went to Poz's on . . . on Sunday . . . no, Saturday, 'cause it was the day of that boxing match. So we went to Poz's for a line and that stupid dyke was there, being sick in his toilet, right?'

Grunt.

'So I tell her to go home because our mam doesn't know but our dad said not to let her go to Poz's until she's fourteen and that's not 'til August but she's such a fucking whiny little bitch with a face like, "urrr", like a cat's arse, you know, you know Bex, don't you?'

Grunt.

'So she's falling off her shoes and her tits are falling out of her top and that's not pretty.' He lights the joint he's been rolling, I throw my dead one away, and we share his cosily. 'Y'know, like, I don't wanna see that, do I? So she starts getting ready to do another line and I say get some water down you, 'cause she's fucking puked up everything she's had in her stomach and I know for a fact all she's been drinking all night is Cherry Lambrini 'cause it's so cheap it's the only thing they'll buy, right?'

Grunt.

'So, she's fucking telling me to get fucked and I say do whatever you want then you fucking slag and she downs some vodka and she does another line, joins in on the joints, which I'm not happy about 'cause she starts talking to Katy, who I'm trying to get with and then she goes and fucking gets off with *Danny* – ' (Danny's Dildo's best friend) ' – and I can see them out the corner of my fucking eye, and she's got her skirt up round her waist and his arse is going at it like that Jane Fonda "Buns of Steel" video.'

I laugh. Dildo looks offended. It clearly wasn't the right time to laugh (and I'm clearly not listening). Maybe some-one died in the story.

'Anyway,' he continues, 'I think, "fuck this", and I go to Poz's bedroom with Katy. And I've been going for Katy for months, you know that, and finally, *finally* I'm in there, and she sucks my dick and then I turn her around and I've got her arse, so fucking hot, and I push my dick in her from behind, not in her arse, like, y'know, like, her cunt, right?'

'Mmm.'

'And I'm fucking away at her and her big tits are jiggling, man, and it's wicked and, FUCK, man, the door opens and Poz puts his head round the corner and goes, "Dildo, you've gotta get your sister, she's well out of it and I can't have her here like that," and you know, I fucking understand his point, 'cause it's his house, right, but if he's got a thirteen year old there, and she's clearly fucked, then it's, well, that's trouble, right?'

'Yeah.'

'So I zip up, apologise to Katy, I go out the room, and there's fucking Bex . . .'

Rainbow.

'Mascara and that shit all down her face.'

Her beautiful face.

'Coke-ringed fucking nose.'

Her beautiful little nose.

'Tits falling out . . .'

Her beautiful chest cuddled to mine.

'. . . skirt ridden up above her pussy . . .'

Her beautiful pussy in my face.

'. . . Danny looking a fucking smug twat . . .'

Me and Rainbow, Rainbow and me.

'. . . stroking her . . .'

Pushing myself into her.

'. . . KISSING HER NECK . . .'

Diving in her, losing myself, opening up, letting go.

'FUCKING BASTARD TWAT.'

Swimming in Rainbow, helpless, resigned, content, forever.

We sit in silence for a while, each mulling over his thoughts. Dildo's words filter through my dreams of Rainbow and reach my conscious mind. 'Dildo? What was the point of that story?'

Dildo shrugs. 'I dunno. Just every weekend seems to be the same, doesn't it?'

I'm looking at him. Poor Dildo, his mop of hair unevenly cut about his ears, stubble sprouting randomly on his face, nicotine under his fingernails, all on a giant's frame. Yeah, Dildo was a gentle giant. His other sister was famous in our area. She was a druggie and died from an overdose when she was seventeen and Dildo was nine. It was in all the papers, and as usual Fez and Troy were questioned, even though they were only fourteen at the time. We still don't know that they weren't involved, so Dildo's never been on good terms with either of them. It was sad but as Troy said to me once while muntered, at least she went out with a bang. The only other way to go here is slowly, when you're old and thin and alone and shafted from working in steel and coughing up blood that you can't seem to get a lawsuit through the courts for. And she made it onto *Look North*. Dying's the only thing that gets you noticed around here. Which is depressing and probably not a helpful thought for her family or the little brother she left behind, all wide blue eyes and black hair and now scratched up from various burn marks and from mucking about on the street on his bike with no one watching him. His parents gave up after she died. Pretty much forgot they had three other kids: Dildo, Bex, plus one other little brother (younger I mean, he's not a midget or anything).

Dildo's looking out across the field to the sky above the art block. Up in the deep summer blue a massive bird soars higher and higher on a thermal, dips forward and tumbles down then arcs round again, soars back upwards with its wings spread wide, through a wisp of cloud, then beyond and away, until we can only see a tiny dot over the sea. I think about what he's said, how everything seems to be the same, always, and I nod slowly. And then, because I don't know what I could say or do that would make anything change for Dildo, or for any of us, I suck another lungful of the sweetly acrid smoke, then let it drift out through my lips, floating away and disappearing into the air.

4

Illusory Hope and My Cold, Tiny Dick

I, however, have a Get Out of Purgatory Free card. The following day Mam comes into the spare room, where I'm on the computer wasting away time I don't know what to do with, and thrusts the phone into my hands, whispering loudly, 'It's a young lady!'

The phone splutters with laughter. 'Thanks Mam,' I mumble, taking it off her, wondering what Ash/Ella/Daisy, none of them young ladies, wants this time. A clear, articulate, polite voice, still with a mild northern accent, rings out of the phone.

'Hello, is this Flick?'

'Yeah, hello, is this Rainbow?' I almost drop the handset. 'How do?'

'Huh? Oh, I'm good yeah! I'm sorry I've been so busy – I've got my exams coming up and it's a bit mental with me being new and transferring and there was a whole load of crap to do . . . but I'm free now if you're free!'

Yay! Rainbow! I think, but I calm myself. The aim is to come off cool, sexy and nonchalant, and also to secure a date and then love her forever and move into a Victorian flat on the seafront at Ness or emigrate to Berlin with our two charming but illegitimate children and I'll be a graffiti artist and she'll be my muse. No problem. I'd better stay calm and collected for the moment though or she'll think I'm a psycho.

'Oh . . . cool,' I swing my legs on to the spare bed and lean back in the computer chair, in an attempt to channel James Dean. 'Wicked, yeah, that's – obviously I didn't worry, I knew you had work so, you know, it was cool, so I'm cool. I haven't really thought about you – it. I mean, like, dating. Obviously I thought about you . . . Anyway, I'm pretty busy too actually. In fact – I'm slammed.'

'Oh . . . so you don't want to meet up?'

'Oh no! I mean, yeah that would be great, I meant – slammed as in . . . well you know . . . um . . .' Fuck. My brain has gone blank. I was so successfully being noncommittal that my brain has lost its commitment to the English language. Think of something, Flick, *think*. I'VE FORGOTTEN ENGLISH . . . *Say something!* says the little voice in my head. What else could slammed mean? 'Beaten?' I mutter. Out loud. Oh God, Jesus and Fuck.

'Beaten? Have you been hurt?'

'No! I didn't mean beaten. I meant . . . beaten as, as, as in tired, as in I'm beat from doing stuff, but, but now I'm free, and not really doing anything . . .'

'. . . So you're not busy?'

'I'm not busy right now, I have, I have, nothing . . . absolutely nothing to do right now. I've been on the internet for the past hour looking up what I'd do on a law degree and now I'm on eBay looking up "smallest", so . . .'

'. . . What?'

'Um . . .' The hole I've dug has no way out. It's dark in here and I want my mum. 'It's really funny actually, um, you, um . . . well you look up smallest and just see what you get, and there's a teeny tiny phone. Anyway . . . I'll tell you later. So where d'you wanna go slash what d'you wanna do?'

'I don't mind, where d'you want to go? Slash do?'

'I don't mind either, we can do whatever you like.'

'Oh no, I'm crap at choosing, I can make massive decisions about my life, but I can't decide how to spend afternoons or what to eat or anything like that. You choose!'

'I'd like to do something that you'd like to do, Rainbow.'

'Well yeah but . . . I don't know what to do here. Go to the cinema?'

'If you'd like to, Bow, that would be lovely. May I call you Bow?'

She laughs. 'You may. But I don't want to go just because I'd like to! I want to do something *you* want to do too!'

Oh isn't she so polite, I think happily as the voice pipes up sardonically, *this could go on forever.*

'Ha ha, well I don't know what we do around here. There isn't much to do. We sit in the centre of Osford and drink alcoholic Panda Pops mainly. What d'you like doing though?'

'Boys.' I feel her grinning provocatively down the phone. 'But for today I'd like to do something that you usually do.'

'Err, okay!' I stop to wonder what she looks like naked then realise she's expecting me to speak. 'Er, sorry, like what?'

'How would I know!?' She squeals laughing. 'What d'you do in your free time?'

'In my free time? Erm . . .' A pause ensues.

'. . . Flick?'

'. . . I mostly just look up "smallest" on eBay.'

'Right.'

We go to the beach. I've lived here all my life and can see the sea from my bedroom window. In summer we have barbecues and jump off the pier at high tide. Our hair is stiff and brittle from years of fucking about in the water and most of us have an obscene amount of bright flowery Hawaiian

67

shorts in our wardrobes, and a wetsuit in the garage that we never use. These are the symptoms of a seaside-dweller. It's normal for me but it fascinates Rainbow. We meet on the beachfront and I grin inanely as we walk towards the water on the wet sands, me holding her hot little hand. We roll up our trousers and paddle in the wash, shyly kicking the water up at each other. We count the boats.

Rainbow tells me about Hull, where she's from. It's almost as grubby as Sandford, but she used to live in a really nice Victorian terrace in a posh, leafy suburb practically in the country, which doesn't surprise me. Her mums moved out here because they wanted to live near the sea, so now they live in a massive sandstone house in the nice part of Ness, right near the beach. That's not to say she's rich. Houses are cheap as chips round here and people from the south sometimes move here to get more land or extra bedrooms, but it's true that some areas of Clyde County have less litter and bigger gardens than others. Ness is considered a wee bit classier that Osford and Langrick because it has tearooms and a reasonable view from the cliff.

She tells me about her little brother, Tim, who is shy and gay and had a rough time with bullies in Hull, and about her mums, one who works in a graphic design firm and the other who writes books on historical figures. The designer grew up in Hull and is of Irish ancestry, and the author is Scottish, with parents from Glasgow and Trinidad. I tell her, feeling a bit lame, that my family come from Clyde County and have for a while, although beyond my grandparents we've never discussed it so I don't really know. She calls me inbred and I call her a cock and push her over onto the sand, and we tickle each other, which is just an excuse to touch. She finds shells she likes and I put them in my pockets for her, planning to bore a hole in one so she can use it as a necklace.

I kiss her neck. We look at the birds together, and try to identify them.

We do the things you do honestly when you're between fifteen and seventeen, and dishonestly when you're older, in the illusory hope that you are still between fifteen and seventeen. This includes talking about life and the future (I don't yet mention the kids and Berlin), our hopes and dreams (I want to get away from Clyde and retire my poor mam from her job on the till at the Co-op, Rainbow wants to live in a beach hut in Montauk, New York, and paint and sculpt like Margaret Kilgallen and Jo Jackson), our favourite Green Day album (*International Superhits*) and also how we both have a secret jones for Gregory Peck after watching *The Big Country*. Then, of course, the most obvious but also most important question, and I've been asking everyone this since I was five with no clue as to how I would answer it: 'What d'you want to be when you're older?'

Rainbow looks to the sea dreamily, already imagining her future, and then a toothy smile slowly spreads across her cheeks and she turns to me. 'I want to be an artist.'

'Really?'

'Yeah, a painter, like I said, out in Montauk.'

'Is there a big art community there?'

'Not particularly, but I'd exhibit all over the world.'

We sit in silence while I think about the sheer enormity of her imagination and dreams and belief that she can make them happen, and wonder whether it's a state of mind she was born with or whether she's just had a lot more encouragement in life. She doesn't seem to be much better off than me, but her mums both seem to be working for pleasure rather than money. Perhaps that's a choice for everyone and I've just never thought about it, maybe because I've never seen it happen before. I'd ask how much money her mums make but I've been taught never to talk about money. It's odd but I've always noticed that rich kids will be like, 'oh man, I'm so broke, this is how much I have in my bank account', and the less-well-off know that it's rude to even mention that kind of stuff. Fucking insensitive bastards. My mind rolls back around to Rainbow and I imagine her in a paint-splashed smock somewhere in the USA, tucking her hair back behind her ears and surveying her work.

'Can you make a living off of that?'

'Yeah of course, it's hard but people do it every day, in every – well, at least in every free country in the world.' She stops for a moment then shrugs without sadness, in a practical, even optimistic manner. 'And everything's hard. If you're gonna try for something, might as well be something you really want.'

I've been watching her out of the corner of my eye the whole time we're talking. The way her lips move, the strawberry pink of her cheeks, each freckle, and I suddenly know that whatever happens to us in the future, I will remember this girl for the rest of my life, that she would change the way I saw the world, and that people like that are hard to find. Practically impossible to find when you've known everyone in your life for its entire fifteen-year duration. And then I tell her that I have this strange feeling, like I'm an old man looking back over my life, and I'm watching this young girl as she looks out to sea.

Rainbow smiles back at me. She nods thoughtfully. 'Like *On Chesil Beach*.'

'Like what?'

She grins, her lip catching on her tooth. 'A book. You should read it.' Her hair whips around her cheeks, both red with the cold, and her eyes look alight and bluer than I've ever seen a pair of eyes look, and vulnerable and honest.

She leans into me and whispers to me shyly, but knowingly, 'I think it means you like me.' She looks to the water then turns back to me grinning sweetly, but almost challengingly, like she's just set a dare, and as we lock gazes her slender arms move slowly, charmingly, to her waist.

She unbuttons her jeans and drops down to sit on the sand and sheds them like skin. She stands up and her jumper and shirt come off over her head as one, leaving a sheer, pearl-coloured tank top and pink French knickers. The top quickly follows the rest of her clothes onto the ground and she hooks one finger in her pants and tugs them down her leg and onto the pile. I'm left still taking in the above infor-mation as Rainbow walks into the waves, turning to smile proudly at me and sinking further backwards until the water swirls around her tummy, sandy at the bottom, clear where the spray splashes at her breasts.

'What?' She shouts in her innocent, playful, childlike voice. 'Too chicken?' She laughs at me.

Cheeky. I can't help grinning wildly and laughing back. 'Fuck you!'

I can't believe I'm about to show her my skinny, spotty form in sunlight. Not to mention it's fucking cold and my knob's going to be fucking tiny. So not smooth. But fuck it. I drop my coat and rip off my T-shirt and sweater. I flick out my belt and rest my hand on the top of my jeans hesitantly.

'Bwarrrk, boc boc boc, CHICKEN!!!' She flaps her arms like wings.

I grin, still frozen to the spot.

'C'mon, Flick. Me and the water are waiting for you.'

I jiggle my leg and bite my lip. I glance down. Yep. Tiny. 'Are you worried your dick'll be small?'

I let out a massive nervous laugh.

'It's okay,' she says reassuringly. 'I'll help you warm it up.'

I look up and she winks at me. I steel myself, whatever that means, and with a last grin at her, I drop my kecks.

'Wooooohooooo!!' Rainbow lifts her arms up to the air and screams and I run into the waves and dive onto her, dragging her down into the water.

She screams girlishly and I follow suit: 'BASTARD it's so cold!'

I touch her lips with my fingers, holding her close with my right arm, then kiss her full and deep on the mouth, tasting the salt water and feeling Rainbow's tongue, my hands moving down further, stroking her back and bum and lifting her up to wrap her firm little legs round my waist. I feel my dick harden. Her hand reaches down and wraps around it. My hand reaches down and touches her between her legs. We pull our lips apart and stay very close to each other, looking in the other's eyes, breathing heavily as our hands explore each other. What she's doing with her fingers feels so good. I hold onto her tight and close my eyes. Rainbow lets out a little moan. Then her hand pulls me a little harder, closer until she's sitting just above me, and then inside her. Oh. My. God. It's overwhelming. She's tight and it sort of wasn't what I was expecting. The pressure all over my dick feels incredible, and going in and out makes the feeling come in waves, building so quickly I have to stop her and wait a moment to keep from going past the point of no return. I kiss her again, and she whispers to me and kisses my ear and my face. I kiss her nipples, keep going steadily, burying my head in her shoulder, thrusting, biting her neck gently and then finally, letting go, totally going under.

Afterwards we stay as we are for a while, holding each other, letting the gravity of what we've just done sink in. Wow, my brain remarks, in a kind of surprised way. You've just had sex.

Yeah, I say back. I know. I smile and kiss her short hair where it ends at her neck, smelling her perfume, still there through the scent of salt and sea. Then I feel fingers stroking tentatively under my armpit, and let out a completely not suave and very girly giggle as the fingers suddenly dart right under my arm and tickle me.

'Oh, well! It's like that, is it? Two can play at that game darlin'!' I dive underwater and tickle her stomach, and she replies by kicking me in the head. I tug her legs gently so she goes below surface and she swims down to my level, grabs my cheeks in her fist, smooshes up my face, then pushes me away, laughing.

We kiss and fight and swim after each other and she dunks my head under and we scream and shout and I try to go down on her and come up choking on salt water. People walk past and stare at us, then one of us will pop up and they'll look quickly away again, at the sight of my dick or Rainbow's tits.

5

Rainbow Time

We walk to Rainbow's place to dry off. It's a twenty-minute walk along the beach towards Ness, and then about five minutes inland. The house is detached, probably Georgian, and made of huge stones painted in soft yellow. The inside is large and bright and covered everywhere with framed kids' drawings in pinks and oranges, inspirational quotations from famous historic people, maps of the solar system. Every bit of wall-space is filled, and I hear my mam's voice mutter darkly in my head: 'There'll be Blu-tack marks.' Rainbow points out the wooden floor they've redone themselves and pads about, showing me around, proudly gesturing to the decoration, which has all been done in the two months since they moved in.

There are photos of them everywhere, Rainbow in her school uniform a few years ago; Tim, her brother, at about the age of seven running a race with a load of other kids; her mums standing with the kids at some sort of rally, the Houses of Parliament behind them, the two kids in their early teens. I realise there aren't any baby photos, then think, of course, 'cause two women can't make a baby. I guess I'd just presume Rainbow belonged to one of them, maybe from a previous marriage or something. Feeling a bit awkward, I say, 'So did one of your mums . . . you know . . .'

She raises an eyebrow at me and laughs. 'Give birth to me?'

I grin. 'I was gonna say push you out, but yeah, that's probably a nicer way to put it.'

Rainbow shakes her head. 'Nah, they adopted me. They fostered me for a while first, but we pretty much knew we were meant for each other right away.'

She's smiling, like it's a happy memory, but I find myself suddenly flummoxed. I don't know what to say. 'Huh,' I manage. 'How old were you?'

'Eight when they started to foster me, eleven when we made it formal. Pretty old really. But they wanted to adopt an older kid.'

'Yeah, babies are a lot of work.'

She gives me a look. 'I think it was more to do with the fact that a lot of people don't want to adopt older kids, so they get left in the system.'

'Oh. Shit. I mean, yeah, of course. Sorry.'

She laughs, and walks into the kitchen. It's bright because it's in an extension and the roof and walls are all glass. Bow opens the fridge and takes out a carton of chocolate soy milk. 'It's okay. You want one?'

'Is it like Nesquik?'

She frowns. 'I guess. We're not allowed stuff like that.'

'Stuff like what?'

'Powdered milk, pop tarts. You know, junk.'

I splutter. 'Junk?'

'You don't think they're junk?'

'I eat pop tarts like they're a food group.'

She hands me out a glass and we toast, grinning.

'So what about Tim?' I ask, gesturing to a picture and getting milk on my arm. I suck it off my sleeve. 'Is he adopted?'

'Yeah, he's three years younger than me and they fostered us both around the same time, so he was five years old. They adopted him pretty much immediately though, 'cause his parents are dead.'

'Ah, I see and they wanted to wait with you 'cause you might have turned into a troublemaker?' I nod and wink at her. 'I get that.'

Rainbow grins and pokes my stomach in a sexy way. 'Well, you have to be available to be adopted,' she says softly, which I don't really understand, but then she floors me with a suggestive eyebrow lift and I forget what we were talking about, how to ask questions, my own name, etc. Bow murmurs, 'Shall we go upstairs?'

I down the rest of my milk. 'Hell yes.'

We head up to her bedroom with no adult interference as no one else seems to be home. Probably, I think somewhat jealously, out at art galleries or some shit like that. As soon as she opens her door I'm hit by the enclosure of floor-to-ceiling bookcases covering two entire walls, packed full of meaty volumes with titles like *The Kennedy Tapes: Inside The Whitehouse during the Cuban Missile Crisis* and *September 11th, 2001: Feminist Perspectives*. I scan the shelves and try not to stare as Rainbow throws her bag on her multi-coloured duvet and peels off her still-sopping jeans. Notably cool CDs in Rainbow's homemade library include *Make Yourself* by Incubus, *Is This It?* by The Strokes and what looks like every single album ever made by the Red Hot Chili Peppers. Notably intimidating DVDs, the titles of which I have no idea how to pronounce include *Y Tu Mama Tambien*, *Volver*, *Le fabuleux destin d'Amélie Poulain*, *La Mala Educacion*, *La Cité des Enfants Perdus* and, intriguingly, *Lucia Y El Sexo*.

I pick up the book about the Cuban missile crisis and thumb through it. 'It's quite cool having all these here, isn't it?'

'Pardon?' Rainbow's fluffy hair springs out of the neck of a bright blue top.

'Ah, that looks soft.' I stroke it. 'I mean, you'd think it would be claustrophobic being surrounded by all these books and that, like the library in school, but it must be quite free-ing, having the power to visit foreign countries and go to different times in history and . . .' I realise how dumb what I'm saying sounds and trail off. She's clearly intelligent and I clearly sound like a retard. Should have fucking read some-thing growing up. Anything. But I swear to god I didn't even really know about books until I was about ten. It just never crossed my mind that anyone would read for pleasure. And then I discovered some *Beanos* in my dad's wardrobe while looking for porn and obsessively read his entire col-lection, spanning years 1975 to 2000. But since then I've not read much besides *Men's Health* magazine and a couple of books on Banksy. I'm not a fan of lads' mags because all the women in them look stupid and pretty much like porn stars with ginormous plastic tits and inflated lips (no I really, *really* wouldn't), so I'm kind of proud I've avoided that cul-tural stereotype, but I haven't exactly progressed to Brontë or anything if you know what I mean. I point at a stonker of a book that pronounces itself as '*the definitive authority on contemporary art, globally, now*', and finish my sentence clumsily, losing faith in myself, the volume dropping off my voice, '. . . to know about art in Guatemala.' I shrug uncom-fortably. I know Rainbow's not making me feel so small and undeserving beside her on purpose, because she's not like that. It's all in my head. I know this, but it seems I can't help myself. I poke some books on the floor with my shoe, fake nonchalance and raise my voice, acting the cock. 'I just meant that it's all at your fingertips, surrounding you when you're asleep. It's insane . . . but y'know, pretty cool.'

Rainbow smiles innocently, unaware of my inner monologue, and nods to the book I'm unknowingly still holding, the transcription of the Kennedy Tapes. 'You can borrow that if you want.' She roughly dries her hair with a hand towel. 'I've got an idea for this afternoon. Let's order pizza and watch *Y Tu Mama Tambien*, it's an awesome film. D'you want to?'

'Yeah, sure, okay.' I shrug.

She slips her hands round my waist and I stand stiff for a moment, but then I fall under her spell, fold my arms about her and drop my head onto her shoulder, enveloping this tiny and wonderful human being, glad she hasn't noticed my awkwardness. We relax with huge sighs into this overwhelmingly deep and comforting hug.

'Rainbooooow.' I let out involuntarily, and burrow my face into her hair with embarrassment.

Then, unanticipated, soft and warm into my chest: 'Will.' And my insecurities slip away and my mind and everything in me shakes with excitement and happiness. I'm such a soft twat. Don't tell on me.

6

Wanking

No story of my life would be complete without attention paid to my most voraciously pursued hobby. Wanking. Spanking the monkey. Teasing the weasel. Buffing the banana, jackin' the beanstalk, applying the handbrake, squeezing the cream from the flesh twinkie, choking the chicken, checking for testicular cancer, wielding the flesh baton, and my personal favourite, slap-boxing the one-eyed champ. I could go on. I've thought about it a lot. While wanking.

It is a warm day in early May, about a week after my first time with Rainbow, which in retrospect, was perfect. Unfortunately, I've spent all my time dreaming and wanking about it, and not much time revising. Our exams are only a month away and Jamie, myself, and Mike have a Maths paper to take first (Josh, Daisy, Ella and Ash take the lower tier paper so, while they do have an exam at the same time as us, it's basically questions like 'If I have three beans and add two, then I have five beans, don't I?' so this hardly counts). To make a long, boring story about inept teaching and apathy on my part short, I'll just put it plainly: no one knows a thing. No teacher seems to help when I ask and no one can tell me where I'm going wrong or what a quadratic equation is. I looked for Mr Banbury, the Maths dude, and found him smoking behind the bike sheds. I give up. I go home. I couldn't care less. All I can think about these days is . . .

'Rainbow.' Her name tastes like strawberry on my lips and I think of her breath in my ear. I think of the gorgeous scent of her beautiful cunt in my mouth. 'Rainbow . . .' The North Sea, freezing, salty, swirling around us as I fuck her. 'Rainbo-oh – yeah – oh . . .'

'WILL?' Three staccato bangs on the door follow. 'Is that you wanking to the word Rainbow?'

I open my eyes and lean up on the bed with my mouth open in indignation. I'm fucking annoyed if I'm honest. 'Fuck off, Mum!'

'Calm down, I were only letting you know there's fish fingers, chips and peas on't table.'

Fish fingers, chips and peas. Because I'm five years old.

'Thank you.' There's a pause.

'D'you want ketchup?'

'Fuck off!'

Retreating footsteps and an 'oh *fine*', as if I'm being unreasonable to want to wank without simultaneously discussing dinner with my mother through the door. I begin to rant in my head but take a deep breath and decide not to let it ruin my thoughts of lovely Rainbow and her lovely smile and lovely breasts.

I'm pulling at my dick again with my eyes closed and for some reason I hear the voice of my French teacher, a staunch feminist, say, 'Oh, all right, cite only her physical attributes! You're shallow, that's what you are, Will Flicker, shallow!'

No, I argue back, her intelligence and mind make her sexy and make every part of her more attractive, thus enabling me to wank in part about her physical attributes, yes, but also imagining them acting in a way that corresponds to Rainbow's personality and innately deep and sincere beauty. So fuck you, Madame Dubois.

I start up again. Jesus. Now I can't get my French teacher out my head.

Then, worse, an image of Jamie appears, saying, 'Well . . . why not?' and hunkering down happily to jerk off to the old bitch. Fuck!

I give up and roll over on to my tummy. It's Thursday at about five thirty. I think about ringing Rainbow, but she'll be having dinner and probably talking about something very clever, like one of her books, or politics, or the mating habits of rhinocerosses . . . rhinoceroes . . . rhinoceri. Yeah, rhinoceri. I could go down and get my dinner, skin my fish fingers and chat about *CSI: Miami* with Mam and her friend Tina, who comes around to share her Weight Watchers double chocolate brownies and lose at rummy, and who'll no doubt have been warned of my 'self-pleasuring', as Mam says in company.

Rainbow . . . I wish I could be with you all the time. To chat about your day . . . and discuss the single currency . . . and slip my fingers inside you . . . hot and wet around me . . . and pull them slowly out . . . and then . . .

Wait . . . yeah, maybe I can wank. Let's put some lipstick on this pig.

7

Choices

So May is chuntering on and as exams (largely ignored) and study leave (highly anticipated) approach, me and Rainbow relax quickly into a routine. We go everywhere together and I start to feel like we could really, seriously, have a chance for a future. We meet up practically every day after school, we watch her DVDs, she teaches me how to say fuck off in French, I teach her how to bellyboard, we spend more hours in bed than even I thought I was capable of, and I feel very grateful and very proud. I tell her things I've never told anyone, I let my guard down more than I've ever done before. Most of the time I'm a pretty upbeat person, but Rainbow knows when things aren't okay and I start to be able to tell her when I'm not feeling tooty-fruity about my life. In particular, she's not fond of the drug-addled part of me that edits Friday nights before recounting them, and instead of being defensive, calling her a whore, turning off my phone and getting twatted, I begin to admit that sometimes I wonder what in the blue hell I'm doing with the precious little time I have on earth.

Rainbow falls into step with my gang easily enough, given that we only hang out with them occasionally because in all honesty now that I know Rainbow and her ideals and dreams and general amazingness I'm a little embarrassed about the gang at times. Putting it plainly I'm terrified she'll realise how stupid and stereotypical they all are and that it will reflect badly on me. To be fair to them we act no different, so I know I'm no better, but I am generally brighter than they are, and not a slag, and I should probably know better than to do all the things we do . . . which I guess makes me worse. In any case, Rainbow is cultured and intelligent and I am not having our budding love life obliterated by the sight of me snorting horse tranquilizer and waxing lyrical about why we're all so doomed. Mainly because I look like a cock when I do. I just don't know if my actions make me one or not (I hope not for Rainbow's sake). The difficulty when you're fifteen is that you have an idea of who you are inside, but you are facing five or six years of time when you will be moulded more or less into the human being you will be for your whole life, and the issue is that you don't know what will make the difference, what will decide who you become. You find yourself doing things you never thought you'd do when you were ten and things were simple and druggies were idiots and you were going to be a spy or a fire fighter or the pilot of a World War Two-era Spitfire and the girl of your dreams was Katie Pool, to whom you said 'I love you' when she climbed a ladder above you in gym and you saw her knickers. And then you have to ask the same old questions, about a man and his actions and how he feels inside, and whether the choices you made were the right ones, or whether they were choices at all.

8

Why Stoners Are Like Born-Again Christians

The tricky thing about stoners, or alkies, or any type of addict, even those of us who do it socially, is that we are like born-again Christians (bear with me, it will make sense). We not only partake in our drug of choice, but we actively encourage others to, we preach, we hang about on street corners selling our wares, we advocate it as a way of life, as normal, even as the right way to be. It strikes me as odd when I think about it, that I dabble in the worlds I do, when I'm really not a fan of the other types of organised religion. And getting stoned *is* a religion. Let's examine the parallels:

1. All religions and all drugs are just another way of getting you high, reaching that heaven, exploring that connection with a deeper consciousness. Amen, brother.
2. Both disassociate you from reality. Example A: While in the laundrette the other day (our washer broke) I read a pamphlet on depression, it being the only thing around apart from a pamphlet from the same series on addiction to prescription medication, and with a hangover and four Tylenol in my stomach I wasn't in the mood for a lecture. I didn't realise, however, that it was a Jehovah's Witness pamphlet until, at the end of an otherwise informative article, it said, and I quote/bastardise: 'Don't worry, because God's Kingdom will restore the "new earth", a society

of righteous people on earth, to perfect physical, emotional and spiritual health. All sicknesses will be wiped out permanently.' Unrealistic isn't the only word that springs to mind, but a definite disassociation from reality. Example B: the K-hole, not something I've tried, though I may well at some point, but certainly the pinnacle of the stoner's version of the sweet denial of guilt and avoidance of responsibility.

3. Both prey on the weak, one on OAPs and university students, the other on impressionable teens and . . . university students (weaklings). In any case, both offer a way out to people in trouble; both are seemingly a solution.

4. Both require dedication and worship. You are a much better stoner if you know the Art of the Perfect Amount of Stoned, you gain more respect the more information you have at your fingertips, you get a better price and better stuff if you shop around and take advice and lastly, perfecting all of the above will enable you to have a long-term, sustainable habit, and not burn out over a mere summer. With religion, the dedication and worship part is obvious. It is required. In the bible. Speaking of which, stoners should get one of them. Maybe I'll write it and make a mint.

5. Both have networks of support. As the church has its congregation, its 'love for one another' bullshit, its interfering do-gooders yadda yadda yadda, so does the stoner. Believe me, you will never have a better friend than a junkie. They will fight for you to the bitter end, they will hold back your hair as you vom into the bowl, they will sit with you at five in the morning when you're waxing lyrical, they are on call anytime you're low and you need to feel that high. And the reason that they both have such fantastic networks of support is . . .

6. The thing about choices/getting fucked up all the time/ living your life by something questionable, is that you want other people to do it too, to reaffirm your choices. It's that wonderfully reassuring concept of 'If I'm going down, I'm taking you all with me.' Aw! The merits of supportive friends.

9

Hubris Already

We are at a party at Ash's flat. It's just a group of us sat about, but Ash is dressed like someone from the seventies, with massive flares, platform boots and her afro wildly curling. The lads sit about and worship her while I brood.

I've been thinking a lot lately about how much puff and booze I'm doing and unfortunately my pensiveness on said subject matter seems to be well timed. Earlier in the evening, on the way over (I came with Mike and Jamie from the chippie) we ran into Gav, bleeding from his nose and both eye sockets. He managed to tell us that he'd fucked up a deal for Fez by spending the profit on skag again. He was shaking and trying to be brave but you could tell he was freaked out.

'It's the junk,' he said with his big grin still present, but pained from the beating he'd obviously just received. 'It's making my head go all weird. I've got to get off it, you know, man.' He managed to laugh weakly and warn us not to tell anyone before the police showed up. He then winks at us, tells the bobbies he doesn't know us and was just asking for money and they cuff him over the front of the patrol car and fuck off with him in the back. The worst thing about it (and this sounds weird but it's the first thing that sprang to mind at the time) is that Gav and Fez are friends. They always have been. You wouldn't expect Fez to fuck up a mate like that. It's a sign that something's getting serious somewhere close. We get these waves of bad atmosphere that run through Clyde County sometimes, 'specially in the reet scummiest parts of Langrick, and in those cases everyone is at risk. You don't choose whose side you're on, or what part you play, someone else does, someone older or bigger, someone with less fear, someone who'll stick a knife in your face or jump you 'cause at the end of the day they've got less to lose than you do. I saw a programme on telly about a place in Los Angeles where kids growing up have to be in gangs, because if you're not part of one then you're against one and you're the first to feel the shit when it hits. Seems like there's so many different places where human beings have set up a society in the world, and they call it civilised and they tell you there are choices, but if you're broke or weak or in need you can move anywhere you like, because you're still broke and weak and in need and the rules all seem to be the same. So it's the same thing here. You're in with a gang or some crazy twat, or you're out, in a really bad way. If something goes down in this wave and one of our mates is called up, as it were, to fuck shit up or be party to something heavy, we just have to turn a blind eye and wish them luck. It's horrible to say but you have to take calculated risks. You defend your family and your very closest friends, but what it comes down to is that you can't risk your life for anyone on the sidelines. And that's something that we've all thought about, and it's not a nice thing to have to realise or decide about yourself, but you can't just act the dumb hero and play anyone else's games 'cause the risk of dying in some places in the world is too great for that kind of thing. And I'm not saying it's as bad here as it is for those kids in LA, not at all, and I'm not saying that girls here have it easy either. Pregnancy can't be fun for one thing, but you can bet it'll be guys like us and not chicks that get picked on for the shitty jobs. But as I say, there aren't any choices. If a storm is brewing, we just have to hold on and keep our heads down 'til it passes.

Jamie and Mike and I agree on this, in fewer words than I've used here, before we get to Ash's. We're all in a shit mood now so, and against my better judgement, we smoke up before Rainbow and the others arrive. The last thing I want is to be on edge all evening and a prick to Rainbow, who, we decided the other day, is now my official girlfriend. Woohoo!

She arrives and the evening gets much better. We cuddle and chat to Ash and the others, who now actually like Rainbow, though not enough to stop propositioning me, and then we put on The Enemy and dance about singing, and we dream and talk together about Rainbow selling her art, and me being a politician, or maybe working for a JFK-esque president on the campaign trail. It's about midnight and precisely at the moment when Jamie whips his cock out for no reason but to show off, and Ash is pulling a pair of scissors out of a pencil case and winking at him, and the room is singing in chorus, when a giant box of laced baked goods (chocolate no less), having been covertly passed around the room, lands on my lap. They look too good to resist, and like a fat kid after a cupcake, my beady little eyes are fixed on a fix. I'm just coughing up cash for a few, however, when Rainbow puts her lips to my ear and says: 'I think I have to go.'

'Really? Are you okay?' I light a fag while Danny, of Danny and Dildo fame, bags up three for me.

'Yeah, I'm fine,' she says unconvincingly.

I put my arm around her and kiss her head, worried about her but still smug with my couple status. It's a novelty to actually take care of someone, and for the things you do to be really relevant to how happy they are. I'm glad to be able to make Rainbow feel good. Ha, thinks my stoned and tiny brain, I'm closer to Rainbow than anyone here . . . so fuck all you cunts. 'You sure you're okay, darlin'?'

'I'm just tired, I'm gonna go.' She pulls away from me and stands up and I follow suit.

'It's cool.' I blow smoke out the side of my mouth, knowing she doesn't like it. 'I'll walk you home. Have you ever tried these? They're not too powerful or anything. It's not like a joint, it's just a little high. We can eat them on the way.'

Rainbow picks up her coat and, without looking at me, says, 'I'm not hungry.'

I laugh. 'That's not really the point.'

She turns to me as if about to say something again then shakes her head and looks down at my hand. My fingernails are yellow and grubby, my fingers clumsy and mis-shapen. She strokes them with her own long, elegant hands. 'Stay, it's fine. I'm not in the mood.'

'Have you never had space cakes before? They're not dangerous, they just make everything funnier.'

She shrugs and looks away. She seems about to say something but she stops, or maybe I interrupt her, perhaps with a little fear about what might come out of her mouth. Coward. 'All right.' I cuddle her and kiss her hair. 'We don't have to, babe. Come on, let's go.'

She smiles and hugs me. 'Thanks. I just don't like the idea of it, that's all.'

I get my college bag and wait for her to go to Ashley's skanky toilet. I look across at Danny, who stands poised, subtly waving my pre-packed bag in his hand. He's done this before. He winks at me covertly, conspiratorially, and I shake my head, pause and then stride quickly over to him, grin widely and open my backpack. He throws two fluffy little chocolate cakes with Barbie icing inside.

'Something for the road, mate,' he says and claps me on the shoulder.

I zip the bag up and hand over what's left of my cash. I suddenly realise what I'm doing, what the deception could cost me. So far our relationship has been so innocent, and I've never lied to Rainbow, I think, guiltily. But then I think of all the crap that blows through here, like Gav's face and knifings and suicides and Jamie, Mike and me getting jumped that summer when we were kids and I know that life isn't like that. Life isn't innocent and me doing two fluffy little cakes won't change shit about it. But it might make me feel better, for the moment at least. So I shrug, feeling myself becoming my cold, stoned alter ego, and thinking, fuck it, I've done them before. And I'm drunk. I turn to see her coming out of the bathroom. She smiles at me and takes my hand. My brain rattles around like a pinball, coming to the decisive point, that she doesn't know and won't, and if she finds out, she'll just have to love me for who, or what, I am. I smile back, kiss her lips, and lead her out of the party and into the night.

I occasionally wonder about these little deceptions, which I've had to do before with Mam and Tommo, usually when I'm too stoned and dreamy to think straight, or muster up much of a conscience. They often seem the most regrettable part of being a little bit of a stoner, but sometimes I think it's all to do with your point of view. In the end, Rainbow just didn't come from the same place as me. She didn't have a handle on things, she wouldn't know when to stop, so of course she had a right to be scared. She just didn't get it, and wouldn't, so there'd be no point in arguing. Eventually I wanted to get off everything, but right now there's not much else to do of a weekend. Ways can be changed later, I think. It won't hurt tonight.

IO

Confessions of a Teenage Dickhead

The next morning I wake up, now sober, and racked with Irish Catholic guilt (and the closest I've ever been to Irish Catholicism before was wanking at *Bewitched*). Rainbow is sleeping beside me, curled in a tight ball and tucked into my right armpit. I'm facing her, feeling like the lowest shit on earth. I ate the cakes last night around 4am when she went to pee, and lay spacing out, staring at the ceiling, feeling warm and good while she slept. That was after I went down on her. Again. My tongue and face in her hot, wet little pussy and Rainbow, legs apart, sat over me, her beautiful tits outlined in the glow from the streetlights . . . Ohhh god . . .

A big grin stretches my face, my dick takes over control of my body from my brain and I instinctively reach down my tummy to stroke it . . . Wait . . . I drop my dick . . . Back to the subject . . . Guilt.

I'm feeling ashamed, scummy and worried. Ashamed that I lied, ashamed that I kept it from her, ashamed I'm such a coward. Scummy because I stuffed them in my face like a binge-eating fat chick, scummy because I couldn't go for one night without getting stoned, scummy because I went behind my girlfriend's back. Worried 'cause I don't know what she'll say when I tell her, worried I really am that scummy, worried that I'll wake her up with my dick, which is now at least a semi and is growing by the second as I think of the night before. I look down at it, poking her thigh, angry and petulant like a demanding fucking child. I *glare* at it.

'Fuck off!'

'What?'

'Nothing, nothing, not you, angel.' I arch my hips back so she doesn't think I've woken her up just to have sex. 'Go back to sleep.'

She murmurs a small, sexy groan and nuzzles herself tighter into my chest. I have never felt more protective or caring of another human being than the times when Rainbow is sleeping beside me and I wonder how I could do what I did last night to someone I care about. I wonder what that says about me as a person. I close my eyes tightly, wrap my arms around her and touch her forehead softly with my nose. She feels like heaven. The word that comes to mind and seems to define exactly what she means to me is 'precious'. I want to hold her like St fucking Christopher and carry her across the river. I want to walk beside her like Jesus and those footprints in the sand and watch her do all the amazing things I know she's going to do. The only connection I've ever felt to a higher state of being is Rainbow. Fuck drugs. Fuck religion. Religion is a drug! I start back on my rant. It's worse than any of the ones we down on a Friday night too – religion even claims your fucking afterlife! Yeah! Girl Power! Etcetera. Again. Sleepy thoughts drift in no logical order through my head. My next one is: look at her pretty ears. They're so tiny and pointy and sweet . . . she's like a pixie.

'Flick?'

'Yeah, babe?' Babe. Why do I always sound so gay?

'You're hard.'

There's a short pause while I um and ah over what to say.

'. . . Yeah.' Another pause. 'I'm sorry, I hoped you wouldn't notice.'

She laughs and I take it to mean look-at-this-kid-he-can't-even-control-himself, which clearly makes me even more nervous.

'Sorry. I get, y'know, hard, most mornings.'

'I know, I'm sure you do Flick.' She pokes her little pink tongue out at me from between perfect pursed lips. She's lying with her right arm hooked back over her head showing a bare white strip of armpit, with tiny dots of dark stubble just scattering the glowing surface. I imagine licking it, and am inescapably overwhelmed with the sheer porn of the thought. I look slightly to the left of it and feel my eyes moisten and blur.

'What d'you usually do about it?'

I look back at her, uncertainly. Now, you have to be careful sometimes because girls ask you things not because they don't know the answer, but because they think they do and they're checking for confirmation of what a dickhead you are. I should know because, being the emotionally intelligent homo sapiens (apparently the singular form still comes with 's' attached) that I am, I do it to Jamie and Mike all the time. Women and I should really learn to use their/our powers for good. Anyway. I'm back in the room.

'Erm . . .' I eloquently banter. My eyes search from left to right for an answer. Armpit – Breast – Armpit – Breast.

'*Honestly*, Flick.'

I jump in immediately with a giant expulsion of breath. 'Okay, I wank.' The three words seem to go down in pitch, like notes in a scale, and my eyes correspondingly lower until I'm staring, unfortunately, at her crotch. 'Sorry.'

'That's okay.' She sounds like she's smiling . . . I look up . . . yep, she's smiling. 'So how do you do that?'

I swallow. 'Pardon?' Keep your cool, Flick.

''Cause I do it . . . like this.' She sucks one delicate finger and trails it down her tummy. Rainbow looks up at me with those whirlpool blue eyes that would drown any man or woman who looked into them, and grins at me sexily. Fuuuuuuuuuuuuuuuuuuuuuuuuck. 'See?'

'Erm . . . Not quite. I think I might need to catch that again.'

She giggles and we lick each other's faces and throw off the covers. Ha! My girlfriend's so cool.

An hour later we're spooning and I've completely forgotten about the space cakes, when she says, 'Flick . . . did you take those little brownie things last night?'

I could avoid the question. I could lie. I could tell her yes and act like I thought she wouldn't mind. But for some reason I can't do that to Rainbow. I want us to be pure and honest and I want to stop lying and feeling so shit and it might be the absolute worst thing to say but now I've left a minute-long pause there's nothing else I could say anyway. 'Yeah, I did. I'm sorry.'

There's a really long silence. I can feel sick rising like panic in my throat. Really chunky sick.

'Don't lie to me again, okay?' Her voice is really quiet, soft and sincere, spoken into the bare mattress, the sheets tangled around us.

'Okay, I promise,' I mumble through the metaphorical sick. Another minute passes. 'Rainbow?'

'Yeah?'

'I'm really sorry.'

She turns round to face me and puts her arms around my head, which I bury into her chest. I can't look her in the eye and I don't want her to see me silently, motionlessly choking with salty cheeks. Bit of an over-reaction maybe, but that's the thing about Rainbow. She believes me when I say I'll be honest, that I'll take care of her, that I'll do my best to be there on time, or find her that movie she'll like or remember to text her. And I know, though I am a dickhead at times, I know I've let down the one person who doesn't expect it of me. And I really am sorry.

'I know, baby,' she whispers into my hair as I wet her breasts. 'I know.'

PART THREE

I

Cocksnozz

The next week the shit hits the fan. It is mid-May, just coming up to the first exams, and in typical Clyde County style, or perhaps just according to Sod's Law, the shit hits the fan *hard*. The rumours have been circulating about what happened to Gav and now we've heard they can't pin any dealing charges on him but he's got community service for possession and the police have Fez under surveillance, quite possibly because Gav traded information for freedom. Which means that Gav's friends are now Fez's enemies. Fez can't deal himself and when we get word of a 'shipment' passing through Langrick it puts the fear in all of us, and 'security' amongst our ranks tightens up (meaning we never go anywhere alone, and hang out in larger groups). So I *should* have been with someone, had a friend meet me, to walk back through the estates of Osford after spending the night with Rainbow. I should have thought about it and not been cocky and careless. I should have also predicted that the amazing life-saving force that was Rainbow would need an equal and opposing force to counter it (particularly since I'm supposed to be taking a GCSE in Physics), but I did not. I failed to see that my girl and my happiness were in fact the calm before the storm. A storm delivered with a certain amount of dark glee, by Fez.

I'm walking away from Rainbow's place along the ocean road when I feel a heavy arm on my back.

'Hello, Flicker.' Fez. Twatted, *comme d'habitude*. That's right, I'm taking French.

'Hey, Fezzer,' I say unimpressed, but cautious. 'How's it going?'

'Not bad. I fucked your sister.' This might even have been true but I roll my eyes, knowing he's trying to wind me up, to scare me. If we were five he would be using the BOO tactic.

'Yeah?'

'Proper hard in the ass.'

'Oh, right.' I nod casually, looking out to sea.

'Yeah, she sucked my dick after and I came all down her face, dirty bitch.'

This is typical Fez talk. He thinks he's hard but he's actually just a big twat. What his claim vaguely translates to is, 'I'm not getting any and I want to fantasise about someone who looks like you but I'm frightened of admitting I'm gay.' That's my theory anyway.

'That's nice, Fez.'

'Yeah, it was,' he drapes his arm over my shoulders. 'So what's happening with you these days?'

'Um, actually I—'

'Yeah, I don't really give a shit.'

'Okay.' I shut up and we walk in silence until it begins to irritate me, testing my semi-faux-nonchalance. 'What d'you want then?'

'I need you to pick something up for me.'

I hesitate. 'What?' Fez smiles gently at me. I knew it might come to this. But I didn't think it would be me, I thought it would be someone like Danny or Dildo. We were all on the lookout. We all knew Fez was being 'careful', which just means he gets other people to do his dirty work. Fuck.

'A little package, that's all.'

I screw up my face and shake my head with disgust. 'No way, Fez!'

'What?' Fez turns and stops me walking, his hand gripping my shoulder hard. He leans in and lowers his voice, speaking softly into my ear. 'It's just a nice little one, a nice little earner, to keep old Fez going through the summer, pay back the debt that Gav owes, the stupid fucker. You're his mate, Flick, don't you wanna smooth over old wounds, make everything better for Gav, make things a bit better for yourself even? There's a fuckload of money in my job, mate. I've seen you. You've got balls, you're built, you're smart, and you fucking use enough. If you work for me, and you need a fix, you want something, you could come to me. Everyone else who could do this for me is being watched over by the police so I need a new face. I think you've got what it takes. Just one package. It's going for cheap and I want to be the one to make some cash off it. You get a dealer, who I'll approve, to pick it up, then you get it off him *quickly*, *you* split it up and *you* sell it on, when I call an' tell you the coast's clear, no one's watchin' and the timing's right, okay? It's a nice little earner. Plenty of the white stuff, and maybe a little methcathinone.'

I look around to see if there's anyone who can save me, then whisper in disbelief, as much to myself as to him, 'Fuck me, Fez!'

His voice gets sharper. 'Is there a problem, Flick?'

I shrug helplessly, hands tied. 'I haven't even fucking heard of it. You're in deep, man.'

His hand moves up to my collar and grips the fabric. He pulls me close so I can smell the mix of kebab and pot on his breath and he spits at me. 'You'll do what I say, Flicker.'

'Or what, Fez?' I shake a little confidence back into myself and stand taller, staring him in the eye.

'Or what? Fuck, that's what! Do you know what happens to shits like you, thinkin' they're not part of the system? You're either with me or you're fucking against me, Flicker. And you don't want to be against me. Don't think you're one of my mates already just 'cause Gav lets you twat about at his place. You're still a little shit and you'll do what I say or there'll be no more treats for you, know what I mean COCKSNOZZ?'

Cocksnozz? No, I don't know what you mean, you wanker ... He's hurting me. I'm looking down at the pavement and holding my jaw stiff as his fingers dig into the hollow just under my collarbone. I want to smack him, but there are people who piss you off and there are people who piss you off, and Fez was one of the latter. Fez was into some heavy stuff, he had a lot of friends. People got knifed, raped, jumped, bent out of shape when they got into trouble with Fez. And I didn't want to risk anything happening to me even just for the sake of my mum's nerves. I was brought home in a police van earlier in the year and I'll never forget the look on her face. I hadn't actually *done* anything, they thought I was breaking into cars when I was just leaning heavily on a Ford Capri, but I swore to avoid ever getting banged up when I saw the worry in her eyes and, later, heard her crying in the toilet. And worse, I didn't want to risk anything happening to my family or friends. Something bad. It ain't the movies, kids. I bite my lip. I think of Rainbow. I think of the other night. I think about what she would think of me, dealing coke.

'OI! I'm talking to you, you little fuckfaced piece of junkie shit. Do you know what I mean? No treats, no cuts, and no girl either, that Ash, or Sunshine, or whoever the fuck you've got. I'll fuck her so hard she'll bleed for a month and then I'll pass her round all my mates, you understand?'

Rainbow. No no no no no. I screw up my face, squeezing the image out my mind.

Fez spits at me. 'DO YOU KNOW WHAT I MEAN THEN?'

Yes.

Fez gives a soft laugh. 'No need to be such a miserable cunt about it, Flicks. Right. You'll get it for me then,' and he hands me a grand in cash, and starts to talk amounts, business and money. Fez fucks me right off.

2

Fucked

It takes all of five seconds to realise it's a bad idea to talk to Rainbow about Fez's proposal so I go to Ashley's the next Friday to sort out my moral dilemma – a mistake from the word go. The words 'Ashley' and 'moral' generally never collide.

The entrance to Ashley's flat is down a tiny, cobbled alley, very Dickens, if you're aware of who that is (and I doubt Ashley would be), all smoke-blackened Victorian brick walls on either side, cobblestones underfoot slick with rain and drain water and the piss of our drunk dads, and then her too-short door, built for smaller people of a more mal-nourished age, the damp old wood splintered and the paint cracked. It has all the hallmarks of an alley you'd get raped down, which might be why she can afford the rent. Ash works in the shop below her flat, a greasy spoon café that almost solely serves things you can put in buns. Think hot dogs, burgers, breakfast baps, chip butties etc. She started there last summer, when she moved, and since then every time I give her a hug, which, due to height reasons, ends up with my nose in her hair, I get a whiff of bacon. It's not completely unpleasant. I love a bit of bacon.

I press her buzzer (so to speak), and hear the nasal sound faintly announcing my arrival upstairs. Someone unlocks the door without asking who it is, and I jog up the narrow, carpeted stairs and open a door into the living room. The flat is a closet, or like a series of closets, the living space just about big enough to swing a cat in. Ash doesn't own a cat, but the neighbour's tom does come by for his share of leftover burgers occasionally, so I might get a chance to test that theory.

I can hear them all pissing about in the bedroom, but no one calls out for me so I take the opportunity to snoop about. Ash has got fuck all stuff. In the living room, there is a tiny box of a telly she got from Woolworths, a couple of DVDs, a dirty couch and various half-eaten bags of jelly sweets. I help myself to a few gummy bears and some sour fizzy milk bottles and head through to the tiny, galley kitchen to find something to drink. There is only one square foot of surface that isn't a cooker or a sink, and it's covered in plain paper takeout bags from the café. In one I find some chips, but most of them are empty, the insides slimed with the brown stains of old ketchup. I open the fridge and find it sticky and well stocked, with the cheapest, shittiest alcohol you can find, basically liquefied sweets with vodka added to it, a couple of untouched burgers, and half a chocolate cake with a decapitated caterpillar iced on the top.

'Why the fuck have you put cake in your fridge?' I yell.

There is some chatting and laughter and Ash calls, 'Flick, is that you or is that a murderer?'

'It's me. Why's there cake in your fridge?'

She hollers from her room. 'It was cut price in the Co-op. I didn't want it going off.'

'You can't put it in the fridge, it's *cake*. It's like bread, you dickhead, it just moulds.'

There's a pause and Ash shouts back, 'I'm sorry, are you my *fucking Mum*?'

I help myself to a massive slice of the cake and dubiously select a bottle of peach-tainted vodka, stuffing the caterpillar's tasty arse in my mouth as I walk through to Ash's bedroom and kick the door open. The girls all scream and hold their hands over their chests, but it's just for show and doesn't last longer than a second. Ash thinks being demure means occasionally cleaning your toilet.

I throw myself onto the bed and watch Ash, Daisy and Ella wander about the room getting their tits out and comparing the push-up factor of Ash's collection of Wonderbras and whore outfits. I know it's because I'm there and I usually get great pleasure out of ignoring them. But today I'm distracted and pissed off by fucking Fez's bastard request . . . or perhaps demand would be a better word. No, wait – threat. Fucking bastard.

'D'you think Ella's are bigger than mine?' Daisy.

'What does it matter? You're both an A cup.' Ash.

Daisy shoots a pissed-off look at Ashley and turns to me, lying on the bed in the midst of a pile of thongs that all seem to say Eat Me and about five black miniskirts, all clearly identical but ordered from best to worst in relation to how fat they make Ella feel. Ella is now anorexic. She asked me a question the other week about low-calorie poppers. The only reason she drinks is so she can throw up dinner.

'What do you think, Flick?' Daisy points her breasts at me with a round-mouthed look on her face that I can only guess is an attempt at coquettishness.

'I think . . .' My eyes roll from her nipples up to the ceiling. 'That if I just get it over and done with, that'll be my debt and bloody Gav's debt sorted with Fez and I can stop taking all this shit and be happy and clean with Rainbow.'

Daisy makes a sound of disgust and turns back to the mirror with an 'Ohh *fuck*-ing *Rain*-bow!'

'You'll get yourself in trouble hanging round with them, Flick.' Ash, dressed as a nurse, with her arms crossed and a defiant but still determinedly alluring pout.

'Don't you think I know that? I wouldn't be here discussing it if all was a-okay would I? I wouldn't be doing it if Fez weren't behind my back with a fucking knife, *would I*?'

'All right! Fucking calm down, I was just saying!' She moves off, waving her fag about, talking smoke and scorn in my direction. 'Twat.'

Ella shouts from the bathroom. 'Flick, we're not just saying you could get, like, jumped or, like, really sick from it or sumink.' She walks in blowing at a smear of nail varnish on a rip in her tights. 'I mean, you could get in real serious trouble with the police!'

'I know . . .' I say more softly. 'I know . . .'

'And you're too soft to be hard.'

'Fuck off!'

'Yes you are, yes he is, yes he is!' They run at me, bras now on, talking in baby voices and tickling me through the pile of clothes. Ash hugs my head into her fake cleavage.

'What will happen to you if you get banged up, Flick? You'll lose your virginity with some massive bloke and you won't ever fuck me, will you?'

'Fuck off!' I laugh, my voice muffled in her chest. I still haven't let on me and Rainbow had sex. For some reason I don't want to, I want to keep it between us, intimate, like. So I cover my tracks. 'I'm gonna lose it with Rainbow anyway.'

'WHAT?' screams Daisy.

'You haven't lost it yet?' Ella joins in with a gasp of interest.

'Of course he hasn't,' shouts Ash over the din, never for one second presuming I might have. She gets up off the bed and pours another glass of vodka and lemonade from a bottle on the windowsill, going easy on the lemonade. 'He's too much of a pussy to ever have sex, he'd be afraid of hurting her.'

'He should fuck you then, Ash, no dick'd be big enough to hurt you now,' Daisy giggles into her Bacardi Breezer.

'Fuck off, twatbag.'

'Don't worry, Ash,' I say. 'I'm tiny anyway. You're not missing anything.'

'Why haven't you fucked her?' Ella, leaning over me so I see the twin curves of her tits hanging over my crotch.

'Rainbow's waiting for Flick to grow a pair.' Ash, at the mirror, applying blood-red lip gloss.

'Sometimes it's a good idea to wait 'til it's right, thank you, Ash.'

'It's better when it's wrong.' She grins luridly at me in the mirror and licks her lips, bending over so I see her ass come out of the bottom of her skirt.

I pop a gummy bear from another random bag of sweets on her bed and retort, 'Taking advice from you on making love would be like taking advice about making chocolate delicacies from a chef who mass-manufactures jelly sweets.'

'MAKING LOVE!' Ash shouts, and they burst into another round of pissed giggling through which I hear the downstairs buzzer.

'All right, all right,' I say, glad for the distraction. 'You can all fucking shut up, the guys are here now and you're not dressed, so fucking get ready.' I hit the button to let them in. 'I'm out for some air.'

'Hey, Flick!' Daisy stops me at the door. 'So, what you gonna do about Fez?'

I take her cigarette out of her hand and turn down the stairs. 'What he says, I guess. Got no choice, really. Fucked if I do, fucked if I don't.'

'Either way,' Ash grins. 'You can kiss goodbye to your innocence.'

3

Teenage Kicks

The next day I go round to Rainbow's to try to take my mind off the deal. Whatever I decide, I think, best to sleep on it first. And since the night before I got to putting the world to rights with Jamie and Mike, and didn't actually sleep, I haven't technically done this yet, thus buying myself more time. Yeah! I'm a genius. I've also very cleverly found something else to rant about to get out my aggression and it doubles as something that will make me sound smart to Rainbow – one of my favourite topics in fact – politics! Yay! I'm so gay. Anyway, I saw in the paper wrapped around our chips last night something about immigration and terror-ism and the same old shit from the *Daily Mail* about being overrun. The thing is, if they were calmer and not so insane about everything they'd be way more convincing. Besides, I like the fact that England is a safe haven for people in war-torn places with horrible lives; you'd have to be a bit of a bastard not to want to be a haven for people who really need it. But there are problems that need resolving, such as integration and certain beliefs people hold that they can't be allowed to support here – the notion that women are worth less than men and are obscene if they show some skin, for instance – and until those right-wing cocks stop shouting at each other the real issues will never be solved, as I explain so articulately to Rainbow.

So I pace her yellow carpet, gesticulating, feeling like a

professor. A hot professor. And she's my student. Yeah . . . Anyway. Back in the room.

'It feels like no one ever fucking thinks about the north or people that live in the country as opposed to big cities. That's why I want to go into politics because I'd do it right. I'd be fucking fair. I'd represent everybody. Everything the news reports these days is about London and people in the south.'

'Mmm,' says Rainbow, drawing on her sketchbook, lain on the floor, smiling up at me.

'And there's so much in the news about religion these days, but most English people are atheists or agnostics, all this stuff is just the people in the cities. What about people who've paid their taxes all their lives and are ignored because they don't have a massive religious group lobbying for them? My parents have worked solidly all their lives for shit pensions and then some woman can sit on her arse at home 'cause her religion deems her incapable of working and then my mam's taxes pay for her benefits so she can have seven kids and wrap all the girls in black. The government concentrates on helping out minorities, but what about the *majority*? What about England *outside* London? Or are we so far north they think we're Scottish? I don't know anyone who isn't an atheist or agnostic or just C of E and we don't have an inner-city school we just have shit ones in villages. And they're all getting rebuilt, yeah, but what's the point of a new building with the same shit teachers and the same shit curriculum?'

'They're just throwing money at the problem without any real understanding,' Rainbow agrees, colouring in a doodle. 'You're very enlightened, Will, I'm glad you're a feminist.'

'Yeah, baby!'

'Holla!' Rainbow makes a peace sign at me.

'What we really need,' I continue, 'is a representative Member of Parliament for our area.'

'Mmm, the government as it is can never be truly representative because the system is set up so politicians generally come from rich backgrounds, public schools and Oxford or Cambridge, and most people don't. Right?'

'Yeah. Probably better than I could have put it.'

She grins and I go off into a dream again, trying to remember exactly what she said and what I liked about it. Maybe I should write it down, but Rainbow writes everything down anyway so I'm sure she'll remember. I stare around at her books and think about how small her head looks and how you'd expect her brain to be this vast chasm where all this knowledge and wisdom was stored and where tiny little midgets ran around working on manically productive processors, taking the information down spiral staircases to her mouth, where those beautiful swollen lips would impart their genius on the world. But it's not a vast chasm, it's a normal-sized head. Hmm.

'I read a book from the point of view of someone like you the other day.' A voice appears from the direction of Rainbow's bum, which wiggles at me as she searches for something. 'I was sure my trainers were under my bed. Now where . . .?'

'Oh, yeah? What book was that then?'

'Err, it's by this really good middle-aged male author, I liked all his other books but . . . I read it in the library instead of going to art.'

'I thought you liked art?' Her gold and green bra is on the floor and I hook it with my foot, kick it up to my hands and rub my thumbs into the silky material.

'I do. I'd just done all the work already and Mr Hull understands if I'm not in an arty mood I won't get anything done anyway. Aha!' She tugs a pair of pink Converse with printed orange flowers on them from underneath her wardrobe.

'Oh, right. So how was the book?'

'Shit. You'd have hated it. I could hardly finish it – I had to make myself. It was written in the first person and he didn't sound fifteen at all, WAY too goody goody, even for a good guy, said words like "cuss" and he was white, the story was too structured for the character, who was supposed to not be great at English and he kept illustrating things by saying, "Oh, I'm finding it really difficult to tell a story," which was so not subtle and obviously the author trying to make us believe this kid was fifteen. It was a LIE.'

I sit down on her bed and watch her pull her trainers on, her legs so much shorter than mine, and tiny like a child. Or a hot Asian chick, I grin to myself.

'Plus he kept saying things like, "kids these days", and I know we all take the piss out of our friends but this wasn't taking the piss, it was done so the perspective was recognisably adult.'

'Ad-*ult*?' I grin at her. 'Like porn?'

'Yes, Flick, like porn,' she sighs. 'I'm trying to be serious here, you're not even listening.'

'I was listening!' I put down her bra. 'It was a joke.'

It occurs to me that there aren't many books written from the point of view of normal people, by which I mean people like the people I know. Thinking about it, it's very probably because no one I know can even spell, never mind write a book/short story/sentence. When would you find the time anyway? Everyone works or goes to school or gets pregnant or is far too muntered. We're all very busy.

But even the books that are written for us we wouldn't read, Rainbow points out, because most of them don't get it.

The authors, all much older, only refer to the naive mistakes and foolishness of youth. They don't want to admit that the people they were when they were young were actually *them* and were, at that point in adolescence, just as important and profound, just as much people as grown-ups.

'No teenager in a book is ever treated like a full human being,' she says, kissing me on the nose. 'We live an apologetic half-life, waiting to be redeemed by adulthood.' I kiss her back. My wise little woman.

'Rainbow . . .' Oh my god, I think, surprising myself. I'm about to say it. And then I do: 'I love you.'

She looks shocked (don't know how to take this – could be good, could be bad) and then her face crinkles into a beaming smile.

'I love you too, Will.'

I beam right back. She bows her head shyly and I pull her close, smelling her perfume (White Musk by Body Shop). We kiss. We look at each other. I try to memorise her face.

We kiss again. And again. And then the kissing continues in a southbound direction. And then I take Rainbow's top off and unbutton my jeans.

Adulthood, you can wait, I think, a warm feeling spreading up my chest. I'm good right here.

4

The Nearest I'll Get to Wimbledon

I think about Fez's request/outright threat a little more that night and decide I better bite the bullet and make an attempt to get it over and done with before exams. So I make the call he instructed me to make and I meet Kyle Craig, one of his contacts, outside school the next day. He's a couple of years older than me but because he has the personality of an excitable child, I always feel like he's my age. We know each other from scouts, when we were kids, and from Ritzies pretty much every Friday, so he grins sheepishly and slaps me on the back.

'Hiya, dickhead!' Kyle's a character. A lively little shit, full of enthusiasm for his two interests: contemporary social commentary film and hardcore drug use. He's irritating as fuck, but he's the only dealer Fez suggested that I knew I could trust to get me the dirt and keep it clean (i.e. not use half of it then replace it with talcum powder) and, as always, to deliver a detailed account of the latest releases on Collector's Edition.

'Y'seen *La Haine*, mate?'

'No, Kyle, what's that?'

'French film, mate, means 'the hate' in English. Ha. Means the hate, mate. Poet and I don't know it, right?'

I grimace as Kyle beams and lets us into his home, just next to the school gates.

'ALL RIGHT?' He slams the back door shut.

'ALL RIGHT, DARLING.' Kyle's mum sits in front of the TV in trackies and a Sandford football shirt, glass of wine in hand.

'Hello, my gorgeous Mam!' Kyle kisses her cheek and sits on her lap. 'How was your day? Fabulous, I hope?'

'Get off, you! Yeah, it was fine. Oh hello, Will, how are you?'

'Fine thank you, Mrs Craig.'

'You still doing well in your exams? Your mam said you were getting all As and Bs.'

'Yeah, still going well,' I lie through my teeth then pretend to be enthralled by the TV. 'Oh, is Browning still playing for Sandford?'

'Yeah, isn't he lovely?'

'She'd grab his bum any day, wouldn't y'Ma?' Kyle walks round the back of the sofa, giving my arm a squeeze. 'Stay here, mate.'

I have a good chat with Kyle's mum while he's upstairs. We talk about football, and her social club.

'Well, Kyle said I should get out and have a life,' she grins. 'It's all right, I suppose. The people are nice.'

Kyle bounds back into the room with vinyls for pupils. 'What's that Ma, the social?'

'Shut up, you.'

'Did you tell him about Colin?'

'Mr Earnshaw,' his ma cautions. 'No, I didn't.'

'She's met a bloke called Colin who fancies her.'

'Shut up! Go and get your mother some wine.'

'It's down by your feet, Ma. He asked her to dinner at the *Italiano*,' Kyle snorts and mimics Alan Partridge: 'Get your glad rags on love, I'm taking you out on the town!'

'Oh stop it, you annoying child!'

I grin. 'I think you should go for it, Mrs Craig.'

Kyle's mum put up with his dad hitting her for years. It's no secret. He left eventually, when Kyle stood up to him.

I saw them all together at the train station, shortly before he moved out. His dad looked like he'd driven Kyle and his mum there, because he wasn't getting on the train with them, and he kept jingling his car keys, swinging them about in his hand nervously. Clearly Kyle was in a bad mood, not happy about him hanging about, so I didn't announce my presence. His dad kept trying to make conversation. Kyle was stony-eyed, standing puffed up, his chest broader and prouder than his father's, who seemed small and much older by comparison. His dad was serving him these delicate, almost shy questions, and Kyle slamming back short aggressive responses, little grunts of exertion.

Eventually his dad gave up talking. After a long silence, I heard him clear his throat self-consciously: 'Your train's here.'

The two-carriage pulled into the station and instead of going for a hug or a kiss or even touching hands goodbye, Kyle's dad stepped away and watched his family board the train, knowing that those niceties, those little expressions of love and affection, are not his to expect. You could see it in his face – he knew he'd lost his son. As I watched him fumble for details of Kyle's life, the friends he had, a girl he'd talked to, I felt how hopeless and pathetic it all was, and sad too, like his dad was broken and couldn't, no matter what he did, communicate with Kyle or his mam properly. And I could see in that moment how frustration at this could lead to hitting out at someone. You only hurt the ones you love, right? But then I thought, it's still his fault. And I stopped feeling sorry for him and said hi to Mike, who I was meeting off the train. Kyle's dad moved out that week, and when they came back from Scotland he was living in rented accommodation in Langrick.

So maybe Kyle's mam deserved someone. At the same time though she had put up with it and waited until her kids started to deal with it for her until she spoke out against him. Whenever Kyle was on the receiving end of a smack his mam would say, 'It's nothing to do with me,' and turn up the telly, according to Kyle, who likes to share stories when he's had a puff. I guess it's all swings and roundabouts, isn't it? Your mam or your dad, passive neglect or active abuse, six of one, half a dozen of the other.

Kyle hands me a bag of the white stuff and leans in to me, murmuring, 'He didn't have no methcathinone, but that's a fuckload of eight balls right there. I'll need nine hundred quid for that, darling.'

'Cool, have you cut it for me?'

'Yeah, nah probs, sunshine.'

'Great. Don't mention to Fez that you did though. He wanted me to but I just . . . didn't know how,' I finish lamely. I peel off most of Fez's bundle and pocket the hundred left. I'll tell him it was a grand.

Kyle's dilated black holes stare blankly at me as he smiles dreamily. He kisses my cheek a little too hornily. 'Happy now, gorgeous?'

'Mint, thanks, Kyle.' I press my lips together and nod at the brown paper bag, surprisingly heavy, with a block of the white stuff inside.

'D'you want a drink, Will?'

I stand up. 'No thanks, Mrs Craig, I've got to be off really.'

'You're not gonna stay and help Kyle do his revision? He could get better from studying with a good boy like you.'

'I'm doing an NVQ, Mam, he don't know anything about

it,' Kyle protests, as I slip the coke inside my rucksack and grin at his mam.

'Well, yes, but he's very clever, aren't you, Will?'

'He's not bloody trained in construction.'

I grin and wave bye. 'Thanks for the stuff, Kyle.'

Kyle turns to me, lapsing from irritation straight back into his stoned young queer voice. 'Oh yeah, sure, babe, I'll see you around, right?' He sounds like Stewie off *Family Guy*.

'Right,' I laugh. 'Bye, Mrs Craig.'

'Bye, Will love, take care, say hi to your mam.'

'Bye.'

5

The Merits of Coke and Pepsi

This week we, and by we I mean my year but not including me, Ash and Daisy, go on study leave to revise for the impending exams. The stuck-up school board isn't letting me, as I missed too many lessons what with skiving to see Rainbow, who, being a year older than me, doesn't have as many crucial exams or class time this year so can afford to be out of school at hours I can't. Also, she seems to study when I'm not there, whereas when she's not there I get stoned and talk about how funny I am to anyone who'll listen, so having a boyfriend doesn't seem to have affected her grades.

It sort of sucks that I don't get time off like everyone else, but on the plus side it'll be the holidays soon anyway, even though we're in school we don't have anything to do besides memorise the answers to test questions and, as I've explained (lied) to many a teacher, I like to do it in my head so it's pointless writing anything down. Another plus is that it tends to be the lazy, slacker-type teachers that get assigned the lovely task of special needs surveillance, so we often get away with quite a lot while they sleep, eat or read the paper. It's surprising how much a broadsheet can shield you from prying eyes. Ironically we are hawk-eyed most by the cross-eyed Ms White, who seems to see everything while her eyes are turned the opposite way from her head. You'd think that would be a hindrance, but clearly not.

In any case, it's not all bad, because we get quite a lot of time to turn our attention to pressing philosophical matters, the kind of thing you can only think about when you're young or unemployed and aren't worn down by life.

So. Not to incite slander, but I don't rate Coca-Cola. I discovered this about six months ago. I'd never liked the taste as much as Pepsi and also I'd heard Coke had aspartame in, which is so carcinogenic (check that polysyllabic monster out) that it's banned in America, so that gave me a weird feeling every time I drank it. I've since discovered that's only the diet variety but I still think fuck it, you can't be too careful. Don't want to support a company that would sell potentially harmful shit in a can, particularly if their potentially harmful shit in a can is the stuff I'm drinking. There are three other reasons Coke leaves a bad taste in my mouth (excuse the pun):

1. When we were in primary they put a tooth in a cup of Coke overnight to show us how much sugar there was in it and by the morning, I kid you not, *the tooth had gone.*
2. Rainbow had a book of companies that had a history of arguably unethical conduct, and it said Coca-Cola, through a circuitous route, invested in the arms trade.
3. And it tastes funny. I mean seriously, taste Coca-Cola – I'm not advocating buying it but wait 'til one of your mates buys it and pretend you're choking or parched – it tastes *funky*. The aftertaste is like the manufacturer accidentally dropped some Dr Pepper mix in. Just a little bit.

'It tastes,' says Ash after I've told her about the aspartame thing and we're semi-wasted in the Geography room, 'like *cancer.*'

'Oh my god, it does.' Daisy has started speaking like Paris Hilton. Yesterday lunchtime at the chippie she was talking about getting a tit lift 'cause she saw a programme on a sixteen year old who'd had it done. I tried explaining the programme was supposed to show how sad it was, blah blah, all that shit about body image etcetera but she just pointed out the girl looked better with bigger tits. Ash agreed. I'd prefer real, small ones to massive plastic porn ones, but maybe that's just me.

From the school gang it's just Ash, Daisy and me left. Daisy, bless, is here because she's thick and, as I said before, she doesn't do the work. Instead she paints her nails in sparkly blue during class then lets people finger her at break near the lockers. I, very honestly, skived my way into it plain and simple, and Ash, who surprisingly does all right with grades though she is less intelligent than myself according to all our test scores, tried to get a teacher to touch her up to raise her Maths coursework mark then threw a book at him when he wouldn't go for it. She got her own back though, inadvertently – he threw a book back at her and was suspended.

'You know what?' says Daisy. 'Mine tastes like coconut. That's weird, isn't it? D'you think they just make it out of anything lying around? Fucking hell!'

'You've got the one with the Malibu in.'

'Oh.'

'Dopey dyke.'

'Don't call me that!' Daisy pouts at me.

'Sorry,' I grin maliciously. I colour in the heart I've drawn on the wooden table and lounge back in my chair, straightening out my tie and pressing it against my not-unattractive chest, pretending to lick my own nipple and giving Ash a flirtatious wink. I don't mind school uniform that much. I think I look all right in it. The trouser fabric's light enough to create a good bulge and the shirt looks quite hot, as if

I was besuited. Besuited? I think I've just invented a new word. Yeah . . .

So, Coke. Coke not good. And then came Pepsi. I went through a love affair with Pepsi shortly after I denounced Coca-Cola. It's fizzier, it has a cleaner taste, and it doesn't give me a headache. Pepsi is awesome. You can stay up all night on it and you will be thinner in the morning, I swear, I think it's all the caffeine or something. The only thing you get with Pepsi is the burned-out effect, the thin effect, as Bilbo Baggins said, like butter spread over too much bread. Sometimes it fires you up, and sometimes you have two cans and then feel so tired you want to pass out. It's weird, but I'll take it over the Coca-Cola headache any day. Interestingly, the French say 'Coca' instead of 'Coke', which I think we should start adopting because a) the word Coke is often used to refer to the Coca-Cola brand so then you don't know if people are referring to the brand or not because loads of places sell their own-brand Coke and b) because you can mix it up with the powder variety which is handy for cover when officials are around since you can talk freely about 'coke', but not so handy when you ask for a Coke and someone produces a baggie and you have to fork out fifty quid because they start whining that they only got it for you, you should keep your promises, dishonesty forces the whole system down the pan, etc. Pushers ain't called pushers for nothing. So Ash votes Pepsi, and Daisy votes Pepsi to vote the same as me, but then I hit them with: 'No, I've gone off Pepsi.'

'What? What do you like then?' They lean forward intently. What will I say? What will I do? I've spun my argument well and they are captivated.

'I now like, and will only drink, the weak water plus mix version you get in cinemas.'

'What? That's crap!' Ash scoffs.

'That stuff's rank!' Daisy squeaks.

'And also I prefer the stuff from the cinema in Pepsi, rather than Coke.'

We all speak over one another and a voice lethargically booms from behind the broadsheet at the front of the room. 'Alllll quiiiiet in heeeere.'

We each turn back to our open books. Mine says something about General Haig who I realise with a mild unease I've never heard of. Woops.

I wonder if my brother and the lads are going out on Friday. I haven't seen Tommo in a while, not since him, Rainbow and me went for a browse at Langrick market, which was even before Gav got jumped.

Jamie and Mike I see in town at lunch practically every day, because all they're doing with their study leave is pissing about on the slotties at the beach and hanging out in the greasy spoon, but I do miss hanging out with Dildo, who is also on study leave but actually studying, and so doesn't meet us for lunch. I also miss my brother, who is a good mate of Dildo's himself, and I decide I'll maybe see them soon and have a few pints. Wet Tee's baby's head. She's having it, by the way, word got back to me through Mam, who still keeps in touch with her. Dad doesn't really like to talk to Teagan. He goes to see her occasionally but it's obvious he prefers to ignore her and hope she'll go away. That's just my dad's really manly, grown-up, responsible way of dealing with things.

Tommo's Dad's favourite I think. Though he likes to tell people down the pub how smart I am (so I've heard) and then come home and call me a stupid shite (as I've experienced). Takes all sorts I suppose. He'll not be coming for a pint with me and Tommo. We try and avoid having too much family at our family gatherings, if at all possible. So it'll be me and Tommo, Dildo, Tee and Nikki. Maybe we'll go out for a roast on Sunday. The Ship in Osford is great. They do really good roasts for three pound fifty. Really succulent, tender lamb with mashed swede and parsnips done in herbs and olive oil. And gravy. I love a roast.

'*Flick!*' Ash kicks me with her high heel.

'Ow. There's a fucking reason why high heels aren't regulation school uniform, know what I mean?'

'Pussy.' She sticks her tongue out to try and tease me with her sexuality. I can see her chewed-up gum so it doesn't work. 'I've been whispering at you for the last, like, *minute*.' She emphasises 'minute' as if it's a long time. She darts in and bites my ear hard, just to irritate me, and I have to refrain from yelling out and slam my fist on her hand on the desk to get her to fuck off. She sits back, and I give her a dirty look and rub my own hand, which I've now hurt.

'Hey, Flick . . .'

I wipe the spit off my lobe with the end of my sleeve.

'Flick . . . *Flick*—'

'*What?* For the love of fuck.'

She smirks. 'What did you do about the Fez thing?'

I give her a dirtier look. 'I had to do it, didn't I?' Ash leans in. She's wearing a pink lace bra and I can see the crease of her admittedly very nice caramel-skinned tits as she points them towards me meaningfully. I look away. 'Don't try it, Ash, I'm into Rainbow, okay? She's my girlfriend.' There is a pause. Ash looks me up and down.

'Where have you got it?'

'Where have I got what?'

'IT.'

'What?'

'*It*. The *stuff*.' She gestures to my bag.

'Oh, ah way, Ash, it's not in my bleeding rucksack is it? I hid it in my desk at home.'

'Woh. Shit – what if your parents find the coke?'

'*Shhh!*'

'Sorry, I mean, the *stuff*,' she giggles, holding an imaginary gun up in the air and glancing from side to side for the imaginary fuzz. I nudge her sharply.

'They won't.'

'Can't believe you still live with your parents,' she mutters mockingly.

'Can't believe you live in such a fucking hellhole,' I say back, darkly, and she blushes a little and turns away, pretending to write something in her notebook.

What Ash has pointed out has shit me up quite a bit though and suddenly a horrible image has come to mind of my dad rifling through my cupboards while I'm out. An image of him showing me a porn mag he'd found in my room and me going apeshit at him. He sometimes comes in and just looks at stuff. It's his way of feeling connected – he can't have a proper conversation with me, so he'll flick through my things.

Jesus. The coke is at the back of my bottom desk drawer, with my letters from Rainbow and all my secret shameful shit, like the blood test results from that time I got so fucked I didn't know what I'd taken, or that letter from when I'd almost had sex with Nikki, or all the other dirty little secrets. 'Fuck. I'd better put a lock on my door.' I rub my hair in frustration and groan. 'I *hate* this shit. *Fuck* Fez.'

'Ah, poor Flick,' says Daisy, who has been drifting in and out of the conversation, looking at us, looking at Ringo, a lad she finds hot, on the other side of the class, painting pink stripes over her blue polished nails. 'All this over some coke.' She smiles at me kindly, without a trace of sarcasm or irony, and pats me on the arm. 'No wonder you prefer Pepsi.'

Christ.

6

Rising Panic

I walk home a little faster than usual after school, take the package out of my drawer and stand in the centre of my room holding it, silently and motionlessly panicking.

'William!' My dad bellows up the stairs. 'Will you be staying in for tea?'

'Ermm . . .' My eyes dart about the room, then out the window to the ocean. That little voice in my head comes back to me, and says scornfully, what? Are you going to throw it in the bloody water?

'WILL? TEA?'

'No, ta, I'm going out. I'll see you later.' I stuff the packet in my rucksack, pull on a hoodie and jump out my window onto the garage roof, then to the ground. I grab my bike and pedal hard round to Kyle's. As I get nearer his house I try to look a little cooler, worried that the police are casing him. They could've easily tracked him through Fez. You don't know what Gav told them to get himself off lighter. And if Fez knew anything about it, he wouldn't say anything 'cause he wouldn't give a shit if I was picked up by a patrol car. Selfish bastard.

I throw pebbles at Kyle's second-storey window like Romeo to Juliet. Then the ground floor kitchen door opens and he leans out. 'All right our Flick?'

'Oh, hi.' I skip over, a bit embarrassed. 'Erm . . . I'm fucked, Kyle. I can't wait on Fez forever. He's supposed to be calling me and letting me know who to sell it on to. But I'm keeping it in my fucking room, which my nosy dad checks.'

His forehead creases for a moment, then he smiles. 'Well, mate, don't put it there.'

'I don't have anywhere else to put it, where else would I keep it, my bloody timeshare in Marbella?' I say darkly.

'What about your girlfriend's place?'

I look at him incredulously. 'Are you shitting me?' I put my hand to my head. 'Do you know what she'd do if she found out any of this was going on? Fucking . . . break up with me for a start . . .' I cringe with panic at this thought. 'Look, Kyle, I need to know what the fuck I'm doing with the stash, I thought he just wanted me to sell it on asap, I can't keep it any longer . . .'

'All right, man, calm down.' Kyle puts his finger to his lips and winks at me. 'We'll sort it out together. All in good time, mate. We're just having dinner now though, so d'you want to come join us?'

I sigh, exasperated but out of options. The problem with problems when they are trivialised is that then they're not problems, they're just things in your life and you stop trying to get rid of them and start living with them. Dealing for Kyle came second to dinner. That, for anyone, is trivial. Kyle, snub-nosed and rosy, like the Artful Dodger, gives me a cheeky grin that I gather is supposed to reassure me. I roll my eyes and nod him inside.

In the dining room Kyle, his mam and I eat in front of a bookcase of dainty glazed pottery figures of Beatrix Potter rabbits. Kyle speaks to me in thinly disguised code.

'What did Fe-nton tell you?'

'Fe-nton just said I was to get the, you know, thing, for him. He said to wait for his word to pass it on, and under no circumstances to call him. Do you think I should anyway?'

'No, no, you *never* do that, mate. Best to wait for him . . . it's the etiquette of the thing, you see.'

'Yes, I suppose it wouldn't do to be impolite,' I say with heavy sarcasm, rolling my eyes at Kyle as his mam bows her head to sip her tea. 'Manners are a virtue in any situation.'

'Have you thought about just not doing it? I'm sure Fez wouldn't mind. He's a reasonable guy.'

I look up at him. He's joking. Twat.

'Yeah, Kyle.' I glare at him. 'I'd been wondering whether 'tis nobler in the mind to suffer the slings and arrows of out-rageous fortunes or to take arms against a sea of troubles and by opposing end them. And then you know what I thought?' I stick a carrot in my mouth. 'Oh whaddya know, I bloody can't – sorry, Mrs Craig.'

'Hm. I'm thinking what we could do.' Kyle wipes his plate with a Yorkshire pud, crams it whole in his mouth then chews for what seems like an excruciatingly long time.

'Yeah?' I say, brow furrowed, waiting.

'Hmmm . . . hmmmmmmmmm . . .'

I look up from his gravy-stained lips. 'Kyle, this isn't funny.'

'Right,' he's laughing. 'Sorry. Listen, don't worry, hand it to me and I'll sell it on, and then I'll take a cut. I don't have a debt to clear like you have Gav's debt so it's policy that I get a bit of money. I'll tell him myself that I am. Don't look worried, the only reason he wants you to be the main man is 'cause he thinks the police are on to me too, but that's bullshit.' He looks at his mam, silently eating peas and flip-ping through a *Reader's Digest*. 'I'm a good boy.' He smiles at me. 'I'm just not as clumsy as Fez, right? I'll get it to Fez . . . borough, cousin of Fenton, and he can clean up his own shit – sorry, Mam – mess.'

I toss Kyle the blow that night and I'm rid of it, then feeling free and unburdened I bike along the North Sea road, fresh but light rain on my face, speeding along to see my girl, well rid of fucking Fez . . . and utterly naive.

7

Crash Bandicoot and a Quiet Night In

It's Thursday night about a week later and Rainbow and I are indulging in a little downtime. In the tense and trembling silence of my bedroom, she opens her mouth and lets my fingers slide fully inside, and sucks on them hard before drawing them oh-so-slowly out, pulling my face close, and murmuring with an especially erotic pout: 'So what's your deepest, darkest fantasy?'

A silence as we stare into each other's eyes and feel this heat pass between us. My eyes flit between her red, open lips, her tongue wet and shiny behind porcelain teeth, and her beautiful orbs of dark blue, bare, where I've kissed off all her make-up, and suggestive.

'FLICK!' There's a loud bang on my window. Fucking Jesus. 'FLICK!'

I throw it open. 'WHAT?'

Fez appears from under the garage awning, Troy in tow. 'You need to do me a favour.'

It takes about four minutes for me to pull on jeans and a T-shirt and walk down the stairs and out the back door to where my friendly neighbourhood dealer is waiting, but with this short sharp staccato list of ordinary movements so many possibilities are strung out in my head that time itself is stretched, and my mind takes off of its own accord to dimensions we could have gone, should have gone, would have gone . . . Mindless and lost in lust and passion, intimacy beyond imagining, sweat glistening on pert teenage breasts, tits erect, legs spread and my own tongue, trailing around each pink nipple with delicate but firm ease, then sliding over each virgin-white rib, down her soft tummy, pulled flat and taut with wanting, switching from a curve to a line, cave to smooth rock with deep fervent breaths. Back to my tongue, the tip floating over the hill and pressing hard into the decline, tracking fast into a canal of warmth and wet, pushing my face deeper 'til I'm covered in Rainbow, soaked, saturated. I sit up, wriggle my knees nearer, grip my dick in one hand and guide myself inside her, stroke my fingers up to her hips, then, taking her weight, pull her curves – her body beautiful, skin white and moist, reflecting the moonlight outside – pull her slowly towards me and, from above, watch us writhe in sweat and heat in the pool of light on my bed.

Outside, Troy, a glimmer of apology on his face, pushes down on my shoulders as soon as I'm out the door. My legs cave in and I fall to the concrete, eyes on their silhouettes in the dark. Fez cracks me in the face with his knee. Everything happens quietly, softly, dangerously.

'What. The fuck. Were you thinking.' It's not a question. 'There's no choice in this. You get rid of it. You don't leave it with the dealer who picked it up when I don't leave word. The reason I didn't get Kyle to keep it in the first place is a, 'cause the fuzz are all over him and b, 'cause he's a little twat. I need every penny of this money to make up for what Gav cost me so no one is getting a cut of this deal, including Kyle. You are doing it because you are such a good friend to Gav you are clearing his debt for him and now you are also clearing yours, and lastly, you're doing it 'cause no one's gonna turn up at your fucking house and search your drawers. The situation has changed so listen. The fuzz are on me. All the fuck over me. So I don't want this shit any more, I can't be involved in it in any way, I'll just wait for my fucking money, and I want it back with interest. You picked it up. It's your problem. So you, Kyle and a few others of your kind, and I mean little twats, are going to deal with it for me. Let me know when you're done, and give me my profit. And you are all checking up on each other. If you don't move it on, I will get in touch with Kyle and ask why. And if I don't get at least two hundred back on this you . . . are dead. So make sure no one else fucks it up either. Get talking to the others. Find a buyer.'

I'm bent over the pavement, catching drips of blood that ooze from in between my teeth, white shirt now spattered with dark droplets, jeans unbuckled, showing the hair at the top of my dick.

'Or next time . . .' Fez grips the back of my neck then changes his mind, straightens up, and I feel the heel of his boot land heavily on my head, bouncing my nose, which I never realised was so soft, my forehead and teeth off the ground.

'Ah-ahhh-ahhh . . .' my mouth stays open, trying to breathe through the sticky tar-like liquid that's coming off my own body. My head hurts so much, tears involuntarily come out my eyes and mingle with the red/black mess on my lower face.

'Next time . . . I'll really fuck you up.'

Someone, it could be either of them 'cause my eyes are half shut and blurred, pushes me over onto my side with their foot. A package falls on my ribs – the coke. Footsteps as they stroll away, down the alley that acts as a shortcut through to the train station.

I taste the metallic bitterness of my own blood filling my mouth. Fuck that twat. Fuck that fucking wanker. I can't think of anything more constructive as I stand up and stumble in the back door. Fuck that bastard. I have to wash my face quickly, before Rainbow sees, before she gets suspicious and comes downstairs. I switch on the light in the downstairs loo and squint at the mirror. Fuck. I look like shit. But on touching my nose, it doesn't appear to be broken and as yet no bruises have appeared around my mouth, though I can see red patches that might be purple and blue when I wake up tomorrow. I hurriedly scrub myself down, sore as a bastard, and stretch out my jaw, then pull at my hair so it is, as much as possible, over my forehead. Too short to help much. I pull off my T-shirt and flannel my chest. New drops form where the old ones have been wiped away and I realise blood is pouring from my mouth. I rinse it out and it seems to stop. I pull on a T-shirt from the laundry pile, temporarily hide the coke in the cleaning cupboard and take three or four ibuprofen for the pain. By the time I'm back upstairs, Rainbow is peering out the window, wrapped in the dirty sheets, still unwashed from the last time she was here.

'Hey baby,' I kiss the back of her neck and stay in the dark.

'Are you all right?' She turns to me, big eyes even wider, searching my face, pupils dilated. I think she looks stoned, then realise it's the combined lack of light and worry.

'Yeah, fine.' I place my hands gently on her hips. 'They just wanted to talk.'

'Flick!' She hugs me tightly and softly kisses my face. 'Tell me!'

'No, it's all crap.' I bite the warm flesh below her ear. 'Let's get back to where we were, hey?' My hand slips down to part her legs and she moans a little and hugs my chest. Suddenly and with a pissed-off sigh I realise this is not going to work. My chest is aching from falling to the floor. It hurts to kiss.

'I . . . Rainbow, I'm sorry, they've pissed me off.' I push her away gently. Even though her features are obscured by the shadows I can sense her face immediately hardening, building a wall to hide behind. She feels rejected. Her eyes search mine, but I'm hiding too.

'Are you okay?' she mouths gently.

I shrug it off. I can't tell her. Can't fuck her. My jaw sets firmly. I hate Fez, I hate this shitty town, I hate the world. So I have to give her the brush off. She'll forget about it by tomorrow. I fucking won't, but hopefully Rainbow will.

'Yeah, I'm fine. Let's play Crash.'

There's a silence. Her eyes fall to our feet. 'Okay. Sure.' We survive two rounds before mutually begging tiredness and going to sleep or, in my case, and possibly Rainbow's though her back is turned, to confused and angry thoughts, eyes open, awake and alone in the dark.

8

Too Bored to Continue Too Bored to Not

A guy dies outside Ritzies at the weekend and none of us feel like going out. I've arranged with Kyle for him to sort out a buyer so I have to wait for word from him which, suffice to say, isn't reassuring enough to lift my mood, and to top it off there's still a weird barrier between me and Rainbow from the other night that I know is completely my, or perhaps Fez's, fault, so she takes a shift at work (she waits tables at a café on Ness pier) and I stay at Ash's on Friday. I read in the paper that the dead guy was thirty-two. He was stabbed twice then hit by a car. So I go to Ash's and chew gum and she talks about how she knew him, through a friend of a friend of a friend of a friend of a fuck.

The usual suspects are there, at Ash's, and we talk about the same shit we usually do. It didn't used to be like this, surface talking and interrupting eye contact so nothing gets too serious. I used to be honest, I used to have intimate friendships, I used to tell Ash everything going on in my head, I used to give Mike real answers and real time together, before this year and smoking weed and giving up on things I used to care about, like school, and finishing all the levels on *Tekken*, and not doing drugs, and not swearing in front of my parents. When did all that stop? Was there an exact moment? Or did it all slowly become normality? It's all getting blurry in my head, not helped too by being pretty drunk already by 8pm. Sat in Ashley's, I think about when and why and how I've changed, and I realise there have been several occasions over the past few years that for some reason I remember more vividly than others, moments where reality just appeared to part and slip a little, falling away from itself to reveal a new shape of existence.

About two years ago, Ash and I started to flirt. You don't flirt when you're kids, but at thirteen she told me she'd blown her boyfriend and then I made a crack about her twat. We continued from there, and where we used to be like siblings, now we only ever banter about stuff; we don't really talk.

I felt like shit one day in a Tech lesson when I had been up the night before 'cause Dad was screaming at Mum and I'm the only one that'll scream back. There was a test in the lesson and we marked them straight after we did them. I didn't get an A. I got a D. That might not seem like a big deal now, but I always got As before this year. The teacher told me in front of everyone that she was disappointed in me, and I exploded at her, livid. I said she should've fucking warned us about the test. I said she was a bitch. I threw my workbooks onto the floor and earned my first serious after-school detention. I gave up. I felt myself, in that lesson, giving up. I used to try so hard. And still nothing came of it; no one was on my side.

I am so tired of this shit, I told myself. Fuck school.

Last October, Mike knocked on my door to see if I wanted to come work my way through all the video games he'd got for his birthday. He stood there holding a few of them and looking like a little kid, while behind me, from inside my house, Danny, stinking like a skunk, approached and said hi. I told Mike I was going out with the lads. He knew what that meant. We were off to Langrick, to Danny's place, to get stoned. I asked him to join us. He said no, blushed minutely and walked back across the estate to his house. Danny didn't notice, but something between me and Mike changed just then, and he didn't come round to my house alone any more. We used to spend hours at the weekend playing video games, or fucking about in the woods, or even doing our homework together. Now I generally just see him with the gang.

In fact, I tend to only hang out in a gang now. That way you don't have any heart-to-hearts, you don't get down to the truth of the matter. I don't accidentally tell anyone I think I've fucked up somewhere, that I think I might be fucking up right now.

Ash interrupts my train of thought to ask me about Rainbow, hoping we've broken up so she could get fucked. I say she's fine then, loudly in my head: I'm in love with her. I look around to make sure it stayed in my head. Ashley's yawning and picking her nails; Daisy and Trix, let out for the night by her boring-as-shit older man, smoke cigarettes; Jamie, Mike and Limbo flip through the adults-only channels on the telly; Ella and Josh whisper angrily at each other outside the door. It did. And I am. I feel weirdly like crying and, less weirdly, like going to sleep, but do neither.

'Here, Flick, check out the rack on that!' Jamie, gesturing at the screen.

'Shut up, Jamie.'

'Someone's in a mood,' he says. 'You had a fight with the fruitloop?'

'She's not a fucking fruitloop.'

'Her parents are both lezzers,' Limbo smirks.

I kick him. 'Well, it wouldn't work if only one of them was would it?'

'Well, these things are genetic. Her brother is too.'

I rub my eyes and groan. 'There are so many things wrong with that statement, Limbo, I don't think I can comment.'

'Bollocks,' he settles on a channel. 'You just haven't got a comeback.'

'I bloody have, it'd just be wasted on you.'

'Yeah,' Jamie laughs. 'He hasn't got a comeback.'

'For one thing,' I snap. 'Two women cannot make a baby so Rainbow is adopted from an orphanage, and unrelated to her brother too, so thanks for being so sensitive. For another, I don't think it is genetic actually, is it? It's not proven in any case. And lastly, you'd know two minuses make a plus if you weren't such a thick twat.' I'm half-joking.

Mike, who has been quietly starting up the Xbox, snorts and pipes up, 'Flick's got his knickers in a twist.' For some unfathomable reason they piss themselves.

Everyone's talking shit and I decide to ignore them. I'm sat on the sofa and I spy a suitcase behind me and start playing with it. I pick up the one and only TV remote, throw it casually in the suitcase and flick the two levers which allow me to reset the numbers on the lock. I close my eyes and spin the metal rings randomly around, shut the suitcase, and put it back behind the sofa without looking, so I can't give the combination away even under torture. I sit smugly on the sofa. That'll teach them all to be wankers.

Nothing. Else. Happens. I walk back home early, around eleven, and play on the PS2 'til I'm too bored to continue. I lie in bed, eat a bit, hate my end-of-the-day combo of skinny chest and soft belly (how? how the fuck does that happen?), do some push-ups, stare out of the window, think about smoking, can't be bothered, roll over and go to sleep.

9

My Family and the World Chess Champion

Mornings are either brilliant, perfect hours of heat and soft-
ness and feeling like you're rolling stoned in a fluffy cloud
usually precipitating a half-conscious wank, or bastards,
where everything is sharp and too stark for your drugged
brain. Your alarm clock gives you a panic attack, the sun
blinds you, and it's so cold your dick shrivels up and dies
in protest. This particular morning, the day after the dead
guy incident, I had slept for about ten hours and, half-
unconscious, was feeling in the dreamy mist of the former,
when I rolled over onto a piece of paper that spelt the latter.

'OW.' A crumbled corner pokes my closed right eyelid.
'What the fuuuu—?' I roll away from it, back into my own
drool. 'Ohhhhh.'

'Morning love,' it reads once I've snatched it from under
my left shoulder and wiped it dry. 'Don't come down naked,
Uncle Burt's here. He's brought his chess set. Love, Mum.'
I squint at a smaller line, quickly scribbled onto the bottom
of the note. 'PS. don't wank either', dash, 'new hearing aid.'

Fuck. Fuckety-fuckety-fuck. This is all my brain thinks
before it shuts down for what feels like another hour but is
actually, when I check the clock, ten minutes. Uncle Burt is
my only relative I know apart from Mum, Dad, Tommo and
Tee, particularly 'cause my parents don't get along with any
of my numerous aunts and uncles, except for Mum's oldest
brother, Burt, who is essentially harmless. He's very clean,

eats according to a timetable (it's Saturday so today it's one piece of toast with marmalade for lunch and shepherd's pie for dinner), pees every twenty minutes and plays chess three times a day, every day, on one of his always-polished, hand-carved antique chess sets. Mam says one day, if I'm lucky, I might inherit them all.

Mam has been annoyed with me of late, regarding my behaviour with Uncle Burt, because (don't laugh), I used to be his regular chess partner. I'd even go down to the club with him, basically a pub frequented solely by retired military personnel, and him and me would batter all the rest of his rickety old navy buddies, who would then shake their walking sticks at me in contempt loosely disguised as humour as I picked up all their cash. Burt used to make them bet on every game he had, but when they got wise to the fact he won all the time, he started bringing in my innocent little eleven-year-old face to clear their pockets clean.

I haven't played with him in more than a year though. He used to call for me all the time and I'd race round on my bike. Now, though, I beg off more often than not. Burt says it's just because I've turned into a teenager and I don't want to get out of bed on a Saturday morning for the club chess-off, but in truth it's because most Saturday mornings I've only just got to bed and would still be half-cut if I got up again before noon. Sometimes I think Mam knows. Sometimes I reckon she must hear me, stumbling in the back door at 4 in the morning. Other times I think she's too busy to notice, ever at Tommo's, or at work, or keeping up with all the American crime dramas on Channel 5.

Burt still comes round sometimes, bugs me about playing, says I could be a world champion. It's not the only wasted talent I've ever had, I told him, laughing once. He gave me a strange look, hurt pride and a bit of sadness. Burt only got to the Nationals, he'll tell me over and over again. He could have been a 'chess celebrity', as he puts it.

Now . . . Rainbow knows me Mam to say hello to, and she likes her, but this is why I don't want Rainbow to meet my family properly. Don't get me wrong, they're all really nice people, it's just . . . they're a fucking motley crew of characters.

'WILL!' A sweet little voice from downstairs. My lovely Mam.

'YEAH?'

'D'you want some toast with marmalade?'

I roll my eyes back into my head and turn my whole body so my face dives into my pillow. Fuck me, I'm knackered. 'Yeeeeeeah,' I mumble, my mouth buried in the jungle-pattern fabric I've had since I was seven. 'I'll come down for it.'

'WHAT?'

I lift my head up. 'I'LL COME DOWN FOR IT.'

'Okay, love, it's on the table,' Mum singsongs back.

When I get down to the kitchen Burt is sat at our formica table already halfway through his toast. His top button is done up, his tie pushed severely up to his neck. He wears a v-neck jumper, neatly ironed dark blue trousers and lace up shoes, just like he reckons an old sailor should. He salutes me whenever he sees me, and he always carries a packet of Werther's Originals. The effect is old-fashioned, endearing and a little sad. I feel bad for him that he hasn't found anyone to love and now he's nearing sixty and retired from the Navy and living alone in his bungalow on the Brighow-gate Road in Ness-on-Sea. But maybe he's gay. Then I guess him being alone is even more sad in some ways. Round here I'd imagine if you were gay you could feel really, really alone. Ostracised. That's right, I know how to use a thesaurus.

'There's plenty of marmalade, Burt,' Mam says.

'Ah,' he says.

'Sit down, Will. There's your knife. Tea, Burt?'

'Ah,' he says. Burt doesn't speak much unless he gets onto chess. We've had some long discussions about chess, me and him, the tactics, the mind games, the glory. Tommo doesn't have much patience for that sort of thing, but I like to listen. I listen to my mam when she needs to talk to someone, I listened to my grandparents (until they died), I listen to Uncle Burt. It's like Kyle's mam. If you call his house she'll never let you off the phone, but she's just lonely. Everybody needs someone to talk to.

'Will,' Burt starts up, harrumphing politely. 'Did I ever tell you about the time I played Anatoly Karpov?'

'Aye, Uncle Burt, you did . . .'

Mum winks at me conspiratorially and we both sit down to listen to how Burt met the former World Champion in a shorefront restaurant when he was on a Navy frigate docking for a refuel in Malaysia, and challenged poor Anatoly to a friendly match. Burt swears blind he beat him, but even Mam doesn't know what to believe. He can tell a tall tale, can Burt, and now with his memory going I'm not sure whether he can tell what's true or not. Still, we've heard the story before and me and Mam chime in on the punchlines, grinning at each other.

It's familial and warm, and I feel a surge of love for my mum and my uncle. We finish Uncle Burt's story in chorus, 'and he would never admit it, but I took the bloody wind out his bloody sails!'

Mam looks over at me as Burt nips to the loo. 'When's the last time you've seen him then, mister?'

'Not long, Mam,' I lie into my cuppa. 'Don't get at me.'

'Why shouldn't I?'

'I've got a lot on.'

'Oh yeah, busy at work is it?' she mumbles sarcastically, avoiding eye contact.

I finish my tea and gasp with pleasure. 'You're not wrong, lass! Paperwork is piling up. Really got to get on top of my accounting, get my millions in order.'

She rolls her eyes. 'Get away!' There's a pause and I know she wants to say something more, but is resisting. I don't know why but she hates to tell me off. Perhaps it's because I'm so charming. She clears her throat and says quietly, 'He's been getting worse since you haven't been playing with him, you know.'

'He could still wallop you in a move or two.'

She giggles. 'Shut it.'

Then she gets all serious and says some stuff about his health, him looking a bit frail, his memory going. 'He keeps repeating himself. I don't like it. He's my brother,' she trails off and looks away out the window, as if remembering something, as the loo flushes in the background. Before Burt comes back she looks deep into her mug and whispers, as if talking to no one, 'Keeps telling me how to bluff my opponent into falling for fool's mate, as if he hasn't told me a million times, when we were kids and since. It's all about body language, he says. I bloody know, I say every time. He's too young to have his memory go. I don't like it at all.'

Burt's shuffling back into the room, and I don't know what to tell her and I don't know how to feel. I guess he has been more gentle and forgetful lately, but I don't want to see it or think about it. I turn my head away from Mam, start to clear my plate, and before Burt sits down, I say, practically, 'it happens to the best of us', meaning 'pull yourself together, Mam'. I sound, for a minute, like Tommo, like a man, like Dad telling Mam to shut up and stop getting emotional. I stick my dishes in the sink, feeling my cheeks turning inexplicably red, and turn back to the table. 'Another cup of tea, Burt?'

'Ah,' says Burt.

Mam glares at me, as if I'm part of the problem. I can't bloody fix anything, I want to tell her, at the same time as wishing I'd given her a hug.

There is an uncomfortable silence while we wait for the kettle to boil, during which Uncle Burt farts, and the phone starts ringing. I make a subtle but assertive dash for it, leaving Mam to fill the teapot.

Family. You love 'em, but sometimes you have to leave 'em.

10

Love Love Love

'I just feel really sad,' I hear a mumble down the phone. Rainbow has hit one of her mini-depressions. She says it's just hormonal but it makes her feel really crap and have low self-esteem, particularly while she's on her period. It's weird that someone normally so perky can be suddenly mildly suicidal. Only women bleed.

'Aww, baby,' I sympathise. Then, maybe a bit too happily, 'Let me come over.'

'I can't, I dunno. I'm in bed.'

'All the better, I can give you a cuddle. I'll be there in . . .' I estimate the time needed to escape Uncle Burt and Mam. 'Half an hour.'

'Urr . . . I look awful.'

'I'll close my eyes. See you then.'

An hour later, because men are never reliable, I track my bike up Rainbow's drive (that's not a metaphor) and leave it leaning behind the bins. I'm always a bit shy about going to Rainbow's, particularly when it comes to meeting her family, and as a consequence we spend most of the time at my place, avoiding all parental contact. Score. Her brother, Tim, lets me in with a shy hello and waves me up the stairs. Tim is fourteen, only a year below me, but slender, small and quiet versus my stocky, tall and loud, so he appears much younger. He goes to my school in Langrick, but I've barely noticed him about. When I have we've shared the occasional nod in the corridor, but he seems mostly to keep to himself. Probably because he's clearly gay, being a bit gentle, if you know what I mean, and if you're gay you don't want to stick your head above the parapet at our school. You might not get beaten up if you're lucky, but you'd sure as shit be shunned.

They don't look alike, him and Rainbow. Well, they wouldn't, would they? Tim's complexion is pasty and pink where Rainbow is pale, but turning an olive-y colour as the sun works its magic on her. Tim has jet black hair, where Rainbow has chocolate brown. Tim's eyes are dark, Rainbow's are blue. Tim is slim, Rainbow seems to come from meaty, muscular folk. I realise as I run up the stairs that Rainbow has never told me anything about her biological parents. Did I ask? I can't remember.

Tim follows me up and softly walks into his own room, smiling sweetly at me as he shuts the door. Whenever I've been around at Rainbow's, Tim has barely said two words to me, but he seems to like me. It occurs to me he might fancy me, good-looking fella that I am, but perhaps that's just me being a cock.

I knock gently on Rainbow's door in case she's asleep.

'Bow?' I say softly, considerate like, and the door opens and one blue-as-an-ocean-erotically-wide-and-innocent-eye peers at me through the crack.

'Hello,' her little mouth trembles. Her eyes drop to her feet and she lets the door open shyly, hunching up her shoulders, giving me a tantalising glimpse of her belly button through massive, pink, teddy-says-love pyjamas. I track my gaze over her beautiful body, face bare and vulnerable, the outline of her nipples visible under her shirt, the pj bottoms caressing the curves of her soft thighs, purple painted toenails on olive-tanned feet. Like a little monkey. I let out what is possibly the gayest 'awww' ever, shoo her back into bed, climb in beside her and wait while she wriggles around to burrow into my chest, before enveloping her in my heavy limbs. Ahhhhhh, Rainbow. I feel hopelessly clumsy and flawless and perfect.

'Ahhhhh you too,' she whispers into my T-shirt and I cuddle and kiss her and stroke her fluffy pyjamas like we're two gay little rabbits in a Disney film. Ahhhhh, love, love, love.

II

Tick Tock Tick Tock

It feels like a clock is ticking in the back of my mind. A week has passed since the episode with Fez and Troy. On the plus side I've had no word from Fez either and if the police are all over him like he says, then I doubt that he'll have many opportunities to jump me. So I might be happy that his violent enthusiasm for the deal had dissipated, I might even feel free, if it weren't for the bag of coke mingling with my boxers and condoms in my sock drawer. But life seems to go on regardless and the coke remains in my room and I manage to distract myself by becoming more and more desperately funny, chatting to Rainbow, Ash and the like about Pepsi vs. Coke, the sad disappearance of the gloopy coffee one in the Roses tin, and Baileys liqueur – gay but tasty. I push the deal out of my thoughts and try not to worry. Fez doesn't want to know the details anyway so for all he knows we could already be doing it. I just have to sit tight and wait for word from Kyle, who I've asked to look into buyers for me, and then get rid asap. In any case, I have bigger fish to fry, as one by one exams seem to be flying past (Physics was utter shite, I aced the English Language Paper 1, and did pretty good in Maths) and then, the next Wednesday, I encounter a day of utter dread and horror that has absolutely nothing to do with the deal or school life. As me mam says, things come in threes.

All the time I have known Rainbow I have been putting

this off. Ever since we first started going out, her parents (who I have religiously avoided) have been asking about me. Rather than tell them that I'm wonderful, they have nothing to worry about, and that she'll let them know more in a year or so, my beautiful girlfriend has decided to completely drop me in the shit. I'm having dinner with Rainbow's mums and her little brother. I chant to myself like a mental patient living in the normal world and trying to hide my illness for fear of being institutionalized: don't say anything that could be mistaken for a derogatory comment, don't refer to the meal as rabbit-food, try not to look like a member of the BNP. Vegetarian left-wing feminist lesbians *can* be judgemental, be on your guard.

Mealtime comes and I'm nervous, chatting so animatedly with Rainbow before we sit down (so her mums will think I'm witty and intelligent, or at least, intelligent enough to form sentences) that I likely resemble Gav on speed, then coming to the table, sitting down and being utterly silent, afraid to ask for bread.

'Are you all right?' says Rainbow.

'Yeah, fine, thank you.' I whisper back. Thank you. *Thank. You.* As if she was an assistant in a supermarket and not my girlfriend, with whom I've spent the last two nights.

There is a silence. Rainbow's Scottish mum comes to the table. I am calmed by her smile, then a panicked monologue explodes in my brain: Asha-Aisha-Eesha-Oona-shit-what-the-fuck-is-her-name?!

'So, Will, Rainbow tells us you're studying for your GCSEs?'

'Erm,' I swallow audibly. The monologue wonders why I am such a tit. And then I realise I should be speaking. 'Yeah, actually I'm just in the middle of taking the, err, exams for them.' Thank fuck, didn't have to use her name.

'What subjects are you doing?' Mum-from-Hull asks. Why do you care? I think.

'Erm. Maths, Statistics, English language and literature, err ... Biology, Chemistry, Physics, Animation, French, Tech and History.'

'Wow, that's a cool mix, I'd have loved to done Animation when I was at school!' Scottish Mum exclaims.

'Yeah, me too,' murmurs Rainbow.

I hear myself say I really enjoy it and tell them we do adverts and get to design our own cartoons.

Rainbow's brother, Tim, suddenly pipes up. 'Mum has a friend who does that.'

Everyone apart from me and Tim is eating, so no one replies at first. Don't say which one, my inner voice advises me, it would be inappropriate.

'Yeah, I do,' Scottish Mum says. 'I should get in touch with him about it for you, you could get an internship, he has quite a large group of artists working with him.'

'They're doing a book at the moment, aren't they?' Mum-from-Hull.

'Yeah, an ensemble sort of thing. You could be involved, Will, wouldn't that be something?'

'Well, yeah,' I squirm, suddenly embarrassed, like when you open a present in front of the giver and don't know what to say. 'Thanks, that'd be wicked.'

Tim starts talking to me about comic books and Rainbow teases him about his obsession with muscular men in tights. We all laugh and I start to let go and enjoy myself. A weird feeling surrounds me. I'm actually having *fun* at the dinner table. With a *family*. The last time I had real family fun at our dinner table was about a year ago when Dad was out and Mum and Tommo joined in with me and Nikki and got stoned and giggled and snorted roast out of our nostrils through five episodes of *Friends*.

Back at Rainbow's hummus and tabouleh salad I tell myself to relax and actually relate my very funny psychiatrist joke well, which, timing being such an issue in comedy, is hard to do under pressure, with erratic breathing being many a nervous comedian's downfall. I am urged into it by Rainbow, who pisses herself every time I tell it: 'It's just the *way* you say it!' Here it is:

'A patient says to his psychiatrist: "Last night I made a Freudian slip. I was having dinner with my mother-in-law and wanted to say: "Could you please pass the butter." But instead I said: "You silly cow, you've completely ruined my life."' . . . Fucking funny right?

Everyone laughs and I relax even more. Scottish-Trinidadian Mum, *Aisha*, tells us about meeting *Lucy* (Hull Mum)'s parents for the first time, which is very funny also.

'My parents were always cool about everything,' Aisha says. 'My dad has always been a real trade unionist and feminist and loved the idea of me being this strong woman who had no need for a man. My mum's from Trinidad and women are often the head of the household there, so she just said' – Aisha breaks out a heavy Caribbean accent – '"Good, you'll 'ave no man to fool around on you and drink away all your money!"'

Lucy laughs.

'What were your parents like about it, Mum?' asks Tim.

'Hmm,' Lucy thinks. 'The main thing for my mum was that there would be no grandchildren. But then we had you two! So now she's fine. She has two kids to buy presents for and boast about to her friends.'

'Did you ever wanna have kids yourself? You know, like, err . . .' Oh bollocks, my inquisitive mind spoke without thinking and now I've started a sentence that can't end without a reference to sperm, or pushing a baby out, or one of Bow's mums' wombs.

Aisha touches my wrist kindly. 'We *do* have kids ourselves, Will. Some families are born and some families meet each other. But it's a good question, and we've talked to the kids about it before,' she says, nodding at Rainbow and Tim, happily shovelling couscous into their mouths with none of the insecurity I'd expect from them in this conversation. 'We did consider having a sperm donor and one of us carrying a child, but we felt very strongly that we wouldn't love a child more just because we shared similar genes or traits, and it seemed somehow wrong to "make" a baby when we knew there were kids already out there, waiting for us.'

There's a pause and Lucy adds, 'Plus, babies are *so* much work.'

'I knew it!' I crow, and everybody explodes with laughter.

This is great, I think. Familial. I feel comfortable enough to just be myself, which is wicked, 'cause I want to be able to be myself around Rainbow all the time. I'm dreamily musing on this when Rainbow snorts up her orange juice (very prettily) and says: 'Hey, d'you remember Kyle, calling across the road to his mum the other day and telling her she was sex on legs?' (Kyle does this – he is weird.)

'Yeah!' I laugh. 'That was gay!'

Shit.

12

Cinematic

Here's one for you, Kyle. A scene worthy of cinema.

Later.

Back at mine.

Eyes wide open.

A long take.

I follow Rainbow into my room, the light dim through the heavy curtains and cheap, plastic motel-room blinds.

The sea whispers outside.

She turns to face me, curling her top round her body and over her head, letting it fall carelessly to the floor, walking backward towards the mattress.

I feel myself moving towards her in the half-light.

She lies in slow motion upon the sheets, long arms behind her head, delicate fingers held in her hair.

Ocean eyes stare me down.

I kneel before her, kiss up her soft brown stomach, catch her eye.

We kiss.

And my hands go to the zip of her jeans at her waist.

And hers go to mine.

Only then do I blink.

End Scene. (At least all of the scene you'll ever see Kyle, you dirty bastard.)

PART FOUR

PART FOUR

I

Please Don't Say Pussy

'FLICK.' Me and Rainbow are out in Langrick, walking back from Ritzies with Danny and Danny's girl, passing a rank little side street when I hear my name being called. A little way down the street there is a white pebble-dash terraced house, in front of which Fez is stood. I remember too late he lives around here. We saw him earlier in the evening, about to score with some girl called Hannah (or perhaps even scoring – they were stood pretty close), so I knew I could avoid him. If there's one thing more important to Fez than business it's pussy. I've always hated the word 'pussy'. In my head it's fine but said out loud it sounds rank. Say cunt if you want but don't say pussy, it's fucking horrible.

So there we are, approaching Fez, me looking for a way out, trying to signal to him with my eyes, 'my girlfriend's here, let's leave this for another time', and most probably failing.

Hannah walks out of the front door, takes a look at us and carries on down the street and as she passes the kebab place, Fez nods after her and says: 'Well, she's a fucking whore if ever I saw one.' With this he flicks his cigarette in the drain, gives me a hard stare and nods across the street to where a car is parked. Its silent driver sits inside. Fez gets in his car and drives away with a screech of tyres and a loud rev and the undercover cop car follows. I let out a massive sigh of relief.

'Didn't he just screw her?' Rainbow asks with disbelief in her voice, which I tried to describe to Wally (some lad, didn't know him, anyone polite or stupid enough to listen to me wax lyrical about my girl would've done) yesterday and failed. After ten, maybe fifteen minutes of trying I concluded that it was posh-ish-but-without-sounding-inbred. He said 'Oh ay.'

And yeah, Rainbow, Fez did just fuck her. 'Fez has got this theory. He can treat all the girls who get with him and the rest of the crowd like dirt because as Fez puts it, he has "no respect for women who shag stoners".'

She looks dubious. 'But Fez is a stoner.'

'Hence the reason he is also a wanker,' Danny says, and Danny and me and Danny's girl nod knowingly.

2

Kill Kyle and Let Kenny Live

It is at this exact moment that Kyle dances Bruce Forsyth-style down from the opposite end of the street. 'All right, Mr Will Flicker!'

Shit. Kyle. Shut the fuck up shut the fuck up shut the fuck up.

'Here, have you been at Fez's? I've got some news about the deal, boyo! You wanna do it tomorrow?' Wanker.

'No.' I eyeball him angrily.

'What's wrong with your eyes? You all smacked up?' He laughs, making hurr-hurr breath noises. My brain rolls its eyes within my head and says darkly: Let's twat him.

'No, I'm not!'

'I was thinking of buyers and there's one at your fucking school man—'

'Kyle, not now—'

'—who I bet could use some blow!'

'KYLE!' I yank him over to the front door of the house by the jacket as he bounces up and down in enthusiasm. 'Kyle, I said I can't right now, Jesus fucking Christ.'

'What? Why?' Kyle looks so dejected I feel like I've kicked a puppy. A fucking annoying idiotic bastard puppy.

I stare at him wordlessly and my eyes slide to my right, where Rainbow is stood. He whirls around trying to see what I'm signalling at.

'What, what? What's happening? Is it the feds? DUCK

AND ROLL!' He dives onto the gravel drive and throws a bag of pills into a nearby bush. 'Hide the stash!'

'Get up,' I hiss, making an extreme effort not to strangle him. 'Get up, you stupid twat.' The others look over. Kyle is cuddling my ankles and muttering something about being a sheep and repenting. I grin at the others, gesture to the lump at my feet and laugh. 'Oh Kyle, you're so fucking funny.' They look away and I grab his hoodie by the throat and pull him up.

He looks around. 'Have the feds gone?'

'This is England, Kyle,' I growl. 'There's no FBI here, you stupid twat. Now look at me and pay attention. I can't do the deal tomorrow. I'll be with my girlfriend.'

'But . . . we are going to do it this week, aren't we? Fez'll kill me if we don't. I already owe him three mini Mars bars. He's such a tightarse,' he moans woefully.

'Kyle! Jesus, fuck,' I say through gritted teeth, glancing at Rainbow who's watching Danny's girl speak but is clearly doing that thing women do where they listen to your entire conversation AT THE SAME TIME as talking to someone else. This is one of the reasons why the female of the species is to be awed, feared and worshipped, gentlemen of the congregation. I turn slightly away from her so at the very least she can't lip-read. 'Schtop whining. We'll do it schoon. I will cawl yew when I get free.' Kyle looks blank. I sigh deeply and grit my teeth so hard my jaw starts to ache. 'I *cawl* yew.' I eyeball him crazily. '*Soon.*'

'Ohhhh,' Kyle nods conspiratorially. A second passes. A puzzled look flashes across Kyle's face then, not so conspiratorially, but more in a loud and clear fashion: 'You mean to arrange to sell it on?'

'FU-cking . . . yes, yes Kyle, I mean to arrange to sell it on.'

162

'Eeeexcellent. Five by five, down hup. On the sly. No worries.' He winks and laughs and finally turns to go back into the house. 'Oh, by the way.' He catches me arm. 'Where d'you get that cut-up bruise on your head, dude?'

I look at him, wondering whether to say, but he'll only find out in a more terrifying Fez way if I don't let him know now.

'From Fez. He said if we didn't move it, he was gonna get in touch with you, so . . . We'd better get it done quickly. I don't know when he was expecting the cash by.' I shrug nervously, eyes flicking back and forth agitatedly to Rainbow.

'Oh.' Kyle looks up at me, seeming to remember something, and with a slow blink of his eyes that serves for a gulp of both realisation and dread, he pulls his phone out of his pocket. The display shows seven missed calls. From Fez. 'Woops.'

3

Home Sweet Home

Rainbow doesn't talk to me on the way home. It might be just that it was a bit disturbing seeing me smack Kyle round the head and chase him into the house and then for Danny to have to pull me off and then for me to lie that I gave him thirty quid for a video game and he spent it on pot. It could also, however, be that she overheard our entire conversation and she's pissed at me. I ask her if she's okay and she shrugs then shakes her head. I say, 'I can't put it right if you don't tell me,' and she looks at me witheringly and nods at Danny and Danny's girl, who are walking just beside us.

'I'll tell you when we get home,' she mumbles.

We get back to Rainbow's and fall immediately asleep without saying a word to each other. It would probably be one of those nights where I lie awake wondering what she's thinking but she's definitely unconscious and I'm fairly drunk so I zonk out quickly. When I wake up in the morning Rainbow is sat on the end of the bed. Her tense back tells me she is quietly furious. I can also tell because when I say good morning she doesn't start talking. We always talk. Constantly. It annoys people. We talk about everything.

I sit opposite her and tell her I'm sorry if she's upset and ask her what's wrong. She's worrying me. I'm ashamed to say it, but I start crying, just a little bit. And I never cry. There's something about Rainbow that just takes away your shell.

I choke, start holding my breath, can't speak. She starts to whisper at me.

'I thought you were stopping taking stuff. But now you're dealing it too?'

'I'm not dealing it,' I answer back, automatically pleading innocent.

'Aren't you?' There is a pause. She stares at me coldly. I wonder how to make the best of the situation. I nudge her through tears, trying to smile.

'Not in the dark, foreboding, angel of death way that you say it.'

Rainbow rolls her eyes and raises her hands in exasperation. 'Will! Who in their right mind would do that? How can you think it's okay to deal drugs and make jokes about it? It just honestly wouldn't ever cross my mind to ever do something like that. I would have to be out of my mind or a complete idiot, I mean, those things kill people. How can you wax lyrical about the NHS being so good and wanting to be fair and represent people as a politician when even by *taking* whatever you take, never mind *dealing*, you're supporting an industry that kills people? Jesus . . . It's just such an idiotic thing to do.'

We sit in silence for a moment on the end of her bed. I'm struggling to breathe, fuming. 'So you think I'm a stupid idiot?'

'What?' Rainbow says, surprised. 'No, Will, that's not what I'm saying, I think you're very clever—'

'Yeah,' I spit. 'Clever in an underhand, deceptive, bastard-like way. Not intelligent. Just uneducated and stupid and ignorant.'

'That's not what I think at all—'

I talk over her with scathing sarcasm. 'Yeah maybe I am ill-educated and smoke up occasionally but you know what, that's just life when you're fifteen. We weren't all brought up in the middle of the fucking . . . country!'

'I grew up in Hull! This *is* the middle of the country!' She gestures shakily out of the window at the sea.

'OH . . .' I stumble. 'You know what I fucking mean, you grew up in some pretty suburb and here is . . . just skanky fucking OSFORD—'

'Don't *swear at me*!' She puts her hands over her face and pulls her legs up to her chest.

'You think these are my choices?' I'm raising my voice now, almost shouting. 'D'you think I want to be involved in this deal? D'you think I *want* to spend my life bored and stoned?'

'Well, you do anyway, Flick, no one makes you.' She moves further away from me, round the bed, closer to the wall so I can't see her face. 'You can say no, you know. You don't have to jump off a cliff whenever one of your mates tells you to.'

'I do actually, because they're behind me with a fucking knife.'

'Then tell the police, get them locked up.' She gets up exasperated, crosses the room, turns around and leans against the wall opposite me. 'By the time they're out you'll have moved away.'

'No, I won't.'

She pauses, looks down at her feet, seems to get ready to say something, stops, and then looks up again at me, defensive and scared. 'What? You don't want to move away with me?'

The question stops me in my rant. We'd planned to move away together, we'd talked about it, but maybe I'd just never been able to imagine it. Or believe it. How could I? No one leaves. And the only time I've been out of England was one coach trip to Spain when I was five. I shrug. 'Yeah, of course I want to but realistically . . .'

'Realistically what?' Tears drop down from her cheeks to her shirt and she asks in a very small voice, 'Don't you think you'll be going out with me in five years?'

'Aw, Rainbow.' I get up and hug her. 'I didn't mean that. You're amazing, sweetheart, you're the best thing that's ever happened to me but . . . Even if I'm not here, Mum and Dad and Tommo and Nikki will still be here. All my friends will still be here. He'll just go after them. And in five years time, say if he even got that long, though I doubt it, I'll only be twenty, maybe we won't have left yet. I've got to make money from somewhere, you can't support us both even if your parents will give you a bit to start up. No one I know'll be safe, and it'll all be because I didn't do this one favour for Fez. Fuck. Can't you see why I have to do it?' I put my arm close around her small frame and rest my head on her shoulder. I lean into her and my lips graze her skin. She smells like cinnamon. Suddenly my gut starts to ache and all I can think is I don't want to lose her I don't want to lose her I don't want to lose her. My voice comes out, trying to soothe her, muffled by her hair. 'It's only one deal . . .'

She sighs seeming to understand, but then she lets out a sob and shrugs away from me gently. 'No. I'm sorry, Will, I can't be okay with this. You don't have to do it. You do have a choice. Anyone could say they've been threatened, anyone could say they've grown up with it, but these are reasons not excuses. You're an adult, technically, in two weeks' time when you turn sixteen, but you're already adult enough. And if you hadn't let yourself get involved in taking . . . all the things you take . . . then I'm sure you would never have been asked to deal anything. Can't you see the . . . what's it called . . . the snowball effect?' She sniffs and wipes her nose on the sleeve of her soft checked shirt. 'I dunno. That sounds stupid but you know what I mean. If it doesn't stop now it'll never stop.'

I run my hands through my hair trying not to blow up at her. None of this is my fault, I think. I hold my palm out, trying to reason with her. 'I've just told you he'll fucking kill me if I don't do it, Rainbow. How stupid can you be to not realise that?'

Bow looks totally shocked and I'm not sure why. She shakes her head at me in something that seems to be disbelief and goes and sits at her desk on a chair covered with cushions. She lifts one up and picks at the sequins on it. She starts to speak quietly. 'Don't call me stupid. I mean it. My parents don't ever call each other names. Name-calling and being nasty just breaks thing and crosses lines you can't uncross.'

'What are you fucking talking about?'

'Don't SWEAR at me! I'm saying I don't want to be with someone who would call me names and be horrible to me because then you'll start thinking it's okay to be nasty and it'll just get worse and worse and worse and that's EXACTLY THE WAY FAMILIES BREAK UP AND KIDS END UP ALONE.' She shouts these last few words in this aching, hollow voice that doesn't even seem to come from the Rainbow I know, but from somewhere else deeper inside her, somewhere she hasn't let me go, and she sinks her head down to her pillow and grips it tightly, curled into a ball like a hedgehog with its spikes out, unmoving.

I don't know what to do. I'm stunned. I'd say I was lost for words, but I'm not really the kind of person to ever not have anything to say. I just don't know how to deal with her, how to make it better. Options fail me again. I go to the first thing I can think of, stunned. 'You said you were fine about the adoption. You said you loved your mums.'

'Of course I love Aisha and Lucy!' An insistent mumble from the chair. 'And I am fine about it, but I'm fine about it because I have to be, Will. That's an example of something where the person involved has no choice. *It* happened and I have to live with it. But this hasn't happened and you don't have to do it.'

'What is *it*, Rainbow? What happened?'

'Don't change the subject.'

'I'm not. I wanna know. Tell me.'

'It's none of your business. You're selfish to do drugs, Flick, you don't know what it would do to your mum if she found out. Or your kids, or the love of your life if you one day had a relapse and they found you dead somewhere, because you OD'd or some cokehead thought you owed him something. You never think of all the people you could hurt. And you don't think about me. It physically hurts to think of your body going through the things you put it through. Your pink lungs turning black. You're just a child, Flick, we're just kids. You don't know, but it taints everything about you and every connection you have with other people for *the rest of your life*. And more than anything I just feel so sorry for you that you think it's okay. And so angry with you.' She lifts her head marginally from her lap and wipes her tears. 'I'm *so angry* with you.'

Silence. I walk over to my clothes and pull on my jeans. 'You know what? If it's none of my business why your real parents couldn't take care of you then this is none of your business.' I sling my bag on my back. 'You don't know anything about this stuff, Rainbow, so just stay out of it.'

'GOD!' She explodes viciously, suddenly throwing her head up and shouting at me crazily. 'Eight thousand years into civilisation, thousands of fucking years of getting high, and none of you fucking drugged-up fuckers have figured out that you stick your fingers in the fire and you get them *burnt*. You're like fucking *animals*. I haven't had to poison my veins with that *shit* to know that it's *fucking bad for you*.'

'Woh, what THE FUCK? What's WRONG with you?' I stare at her incredulously. She's lost her mind. What the hell? 'I'm leaving.' I pick up my jacket and open her door and she runs to it and shoves it shut and pushes me into the wall so my head cracks on it.

'THEY WERE FUCKING JUNKIES LIKE YOU, ALL RIGHT? MY REAL PARENTS WERE JUNK-IES *JUST LIKE YOU*.' She freezes, immobilized by her own words, and puts her hands over her eyes.

We stand in silence for what might be five minutes. Then I move slowly towards her and reach for her.

'No. No. Get out please. I want you to get out of my house.'

'But—'

'I don't want a stupid junkie in my house, FUCK OFF.'

'Fine.' I open the door again. 'I will fuck off then.'

I open the door and she lets out a coarse sob. 'Flick!'

'I didn't know that about your parents,' I pause at her door. 'But I'm not being called stupid, I'm not being called a junkie, I've never even *done* heroin, and I'm not being compared to an animal . . .' I wipe away tears feeling strangely embarrassed by her admission. I watch her tiny solid form and try to imagine how lonely it must feel to be connected to no one. 'Rainbow. I'm not *going* going, I'm just . . . going for now. I love you,' I mutter. Then I leave her, standing in her purple jammies and slipper socks by her overflowing bookcases and half-finished paintings, a small, unmoving, lonely figure with two hands pressed childishly over a griev-ing, tear-soaked face.

4

Funk and Other Genres

I take myself out for a walk. I reflect badly when I'm in a funk. I'm still in shock, but I'm also pissed off at being accused of so many things. The new information about Rainbow's adoption has sent me reeling and my brain is busy slotting it into our mutual history, looking for clues to it in how she acts, adjusting the Rainbow of the last four months to fit the Rainbow I know now. She's a different person now. But even the fact of what her parents are doesn't change how lovely she has been to me, or this blamelessness and innocence and the childlike quality she radiates, instinctually, as a person, or how I feel about her.

I power march for six blocks before I'm out of breath and have to slow down. I come to a stop at a building I recognise that meant something last year, though I can't remember what. A Cherokee jeep crawls past me and the woman in it looks at my face before accelerating away. Not really a compliment when people do that. Was someone killed in the house last year? No, bit severe. Rainbow's face flashes before me. Wait, it was a girl who lived there, a few years older than me. She committed suicide by throwing herself onto the tracks next to Green Lane. That was it. I crack my fingers, glad to be confident of something.

'Yeah, fucking right.'

A passing old biddy and her dog hear me and I realise this is perhaps a bit inappropriate. I blush red in patches, square my shoulders as if to look cool and mumble, 'Sorry'.

I bite my tongue for no apparent reason. It hurts. What did she mean, feel sorry for me? That I'm an animal? Does she *pity* me? Does she think I'm just like them? I guess that's how she sees me now. After the fight . . . well, it doesn't look too good for Rainbow and Flick, and this thought makes me feel ashamed and ridiculous. How could I have let something so good get so fucked up? It was the dealing that started it. But I *know* I have no choice and she doesn't understand 'cause she doesn't know what Fez could do. I can't shake the feeling that this is not entirely my fault. I plead crossed wires, your honour, breakdown in communication. We were speaking different languages, because we grew up in different places with different people and different values. Told you. It's like a fucking religion. Your honour, please see my comparison of stoners and religious fanatics. I am also the esteemed author of the Stoner's Bible (™ and © William S. Flicker 2009). The text will tell you where I went wrong. Not knowing the Art of the Right Amount, ironically.

I kick the kerb and stare out towards the train station wondering where I could escape to. Fuck. Fuck shit fuck. Now the pressure is on from Fez and from Rainbow and I'm closing my eyes so I can't see all the shit that's about to happen, but it's racing towards me like fate, like a story written and set in stone by somebody else a long time ago. By politicians and educators and the feudal system and capitalism and I don't know what. By drug-pushers and dealers and people on the other side of the world in Colombia, wondering how they could make a bit of money. By my friends and their friends and their older brothers and sisters who didn't want to fuck up alone, who didn't mind who they took down with them as long as they weren't alone doing it. Maybe I should never have gone out with Rainbow. Maybe

I knew all along that what I really wanted to do was drag her down with me.

Since everything's falling apart anyway I might as well go get stoned and get the bastard deal over with, 'cause that's what I bloody feel like doing, and I guess that's who I am. Just a little shit who made the wrong choices. I realise with a funny tightening feeling in my jaw that the voice in my head sounds like my dad's. Shudder. Maybe what I really am is a little shit who didn't have choices. Jury is out on that one. My throat tastes weird. It hurts to swallow. Maybe I'm sick.

The voice in my head rolls its metaphysical eyes again (seems to be habit these days). Flick, it says disdainfully, you can't bunk off the deal or beg off sorting out your problems with your girlfriend because you're sick. What you going to do? Give both Rainbow and Fez a note from your mum? This isn't primary school.

I can't order my thoughts so I sit down on a low brick wall and have a bit of a think. I watch the gulls flying overhead. The sky's light grey, the salt from the sea comes in on the breeze. It's that good kind of summery cold.

Right. I love Rainbow. Yes. I do. And I'm pissed off that she said those things, but I could understand why. She was upset about her adoption and about me dealing and fair enough, because I don't want me to deal either. And it *is* taking it too far, I agree with her. But it's not something I can solve now. I've got to give her some time, give me some time to figure out what to say. Sort out all the Fez-related crap. Get the deal done with, so I can stop feeling like there's this black cloud over me, and then maybe I'd stop sniping at Rainbow so much. Maybe I could stop using and she would love me again. Or if I could just keep whatever I personally took on the low, say Fridays at Ash's, then it would never enter the me-and-Rainbow zone and we wouldn't have a problem.

Fucking hell. A year ago I felt like she did about everything. I'm not like the others. I don't come from a terrible home, there's a lot of love in it. But then maybe nobody else comes from a terrible home either and it just looks to me like they do 'cause I only see them in public. Even Kyle has his tea with his mam at the table. And we do too. My mam and dad and me. Well, we have it in front of the telly but it's the same thing. Family time. But then it's a stupid idea that the breakdown of the nuclear family is the root cause of all our problems, 'cause look at Rainbow's family. They're not 'normal' as such and she's pretty perfect, even about the adoption, 'cause she just gets on with life. She is so fucking lovely. I guess maybe we just have to accept at some point that our problems are our own fault and start dealing with them. That's what's wrong with the media and politics these days. Everyone spends so much time laying blame they never solve the problem. I fucking hate Rupert Murdoch.

So I never wanted to be a druggie but once you're there it's so hard to stop when you know you could be having a good time instead of a shit one. Life is so much funnier when you're a stoner. Life without all the shit we take is way too fucking serious. If I was fucked up right now, I think, I wouldn't be this bothered about what Rainbow said about me being a junkie. I would laugh at her.

But then isn't that weird? That I wouldn't be that bothered? Is that giving up on life? 'But what other fucking options do I have?' I say out loud. If I stay basically clean and that means 'embracing life', well how the fuck do I do that? I'm not going to go to uni, 'cause even if I could get in, me mam needs someone to earn the money and to help her and me dad in their old age and that starts pretty soon. I want to retire me mam. She's worked so hard and she never buys anything for herself, never. So that means I'm stuck in Osford, or maybe I'll move to Langrick with the wage from my menial tertiary-level job. And then how do you embrace life in Langrick? Bingo? I guess I could get gym membership if I didn't spend so much on pot.

Right, I decide. I'm sick of waiting. We do it now or not at all. Me and Kyle and we'll get a few of the boys together. You can run into some really hard gangs when you do this kind of thing and I don't fancy it being just the two of us. Now the thing is, who would be able, and would want to, buy it off us? This is like a fucking property chain. Only where are the Kirstie Allsopp and Phil Spencer of our world? The only person I can think of who would be able to get rid of it is Grant, who works at our school, probably the guy Kyle was alluding to when I saw him at Fez's. Shouldn't be too tricky to get to him as I know he's there at the moment doing refurbishments. The school got a lot of money to be done up recently so everything's changing just in time for me to be gone and I do wonder occasionally if they did that on purpose. Only what's changing is that the buildings will be shiny and new and we'll have better computers. The teachers remain the same. Which I think is pretty ridiculous, considering people can go to school in bleakest poverty and mud huts in Africa and still become lawyers. Less chance of it happening, but what I'm saying is that it's the *teaching* and the *learning* that counts and not where you do it. But sod it, we always complain everything in our school is so shite anyway. For instance, the walls in our school are so thin that back when Kyle was there he was swinging on the hangers in the changing rooms and put both his feet in the wall up to the knee. True story.

I drag my reluctant brain back to the topic in hand.

Getting the deal done. Over with, so me and Rainbow stand a chance and so I have something to say to her when she accuses me of dealing. Something along the lines of 'I'm not' should do it.

My phone rings in my pocket, eliciting a pleasing tingle. I pull it out and look down at the screen. It's Kyle.

All right then, I think. No time like the present.

5

Let's Do This Then

Grant is spraying his tag on the back wall of the science labs when Kyle, Dildo, Danny and myself show up the next day. I asked Mike and Jamie to come along, but both of them made excuses, giving me sideways looks that said they weren't into the new me, into what I was doing. 'I have no fucking choice,' I told Mike, giving him the finger as he smirked and walked off, schoolbooks under his arm.

Grant did his GCSEs five years ago. The only subject he passed was Art, so now he does a sideline in graffiti while pursuing his other career as the school's assistant caretaker. Twelve years of education, and he's *assistant* caretaker. And people wonder why I don't bother.

'Hey, our lads,' he greets us as we approach, Blues Brothers-like, from the field. 'How's it going?'

'Straitjackets, Grant,' Kyle shirks his shoulders, gangster-stylee, having got it into his head that he's George Jung. 'Straitjackets and a lack of eyesight.'

I try not to look confused.

Grant nods knowingly. 'Oh aye.'

'Got some going for a song.'

'Yeah? What kind of song?'

'Fairly high-pitched, but for enjoyment of epic proportions.'

Grant laughs loudly, leaving a long and careful silence in the air as he drops his spray can and turns to look at us. Dildo, Danny and me, the team, make a shaky supporting wall behind Kyle, looking down uncomfortably at the ground and exchanging quick and awkward glances. Kyle stands at the front, his nervous energy shaking his knee, for once completely focused on the task in hand. He always did fancy himself a main player. Now I reckon he sees his chance to bag a lead role, to be the godfather, James Dean, the mafia boss with the million-dollar deal. The truth is, he's closer to Sickboy with his lucky break. And it's plainly visible to Grant.

'You lads aren't the first to play this game y'know . . . going to get your fingers burnt.' He surveys his work and smiles to himself. 'I'm not dealing that type of hand any more, Kyle. Girlfriend's having a baby, parents getting old . . .' I'm thinking about congratulating Grant on his kid when our eyes meet. It's for just a second, but I see him accept me as one of this group, part of the circuit. The thing I register on his face, more than anything, is the lack of surprise. Last year I wouldn't have been here. This year, I'm one of the guys. I look away, blindsided by some strange emotion in me, that I know I felt earlier, with Rainbow. Confusion, tinged with anger, tinged with shame. Fuck him. Grant picks up a can of paint and looks thoughtful. 'Time to grow up, you know.'

Kyle shrugs gamely and, as he turns and we follow suit, let's out a cool murmur: 'Oh aye then. Hope that goes well for you, Grant.'

'Looking forward to it, Kyle. Looking forward to it.'

We leave him happily adding black to the edges of a neon man-size 'G' and stroll, hands in pockets, through the school grounds towards the centre of town.

'What the fuck are we gonna do now?' Any reply to Dildo's frustrated outburst is abruptly interrupted by Miss P, the Geography teacher, who most of the guys hate 'cause she's the fittest of the teachers but she won't flirt with us – the spoil-sport. Kyle says it's 'cause redheads are tricky. I say I feel sorry for her, with all of us drooling over her. Imagine the amount of wank wasted on poor Miss P. Imagine her, having to imagine it. Anyway, she's walking our way, carrying some papers and heading for her car, and shrieking at us from across the car park.

'LADS!' She comes to a rest just in front of us, hand on her hip. '*What* are you up to?'

Everyone looks around and opens their mouths as if to speak. No one does and ten awkward seconds pass before I sigh in exasperation and, avoiding her eye but also with confidence 'cause I'm very good at lying (I damn well am), say dismissively, 'Nothing, Miss P.'

'Firstly, Mr Flicker, it is Miss Preston, secondly, it's a Sunday, and *thirdly* you're all wearing identical dark sunglasses!'

Admittedly we probably shouldn't have stopped to buy them – looking round I can see now how it makes us more conspicuous.

'And *you*' – she points at Kyle and Danny – 'don't even *go* to school here!' They look at each other and shift their feet. 'Well, go on! Move!' She flaps at us and we sheepishly scatter and half-run across the concrete 'til we're all out the gate and we rejoin laughing.

Kyle lets out a 'mwa-HAA!' and following it, 'That was fucking funny.'

'So fucking Clyde,' I inject. 'We try to do a drug deal and we're stopped by a Geography teacher!' We all stand there, bent over, pissing ourselves for the next couple of minutes. We're laughing too wildly and our eyes are too bright. I get the feeling that it's something like desperation, like a breath held that finally comes out in an unsteady swoop, or choking on a joke at a funeral. We eventually stop and end up staring out to sea, out at the boats queuing up to dock in the harbour. They can be there for two days sometimes. When I was little our nan used to take me and Tommo and Teagan out to sit on a bench just in front of the beach and we'd watch them come in. We'd make a game of it. Whoever's boat got in first won. Only because they took days sometimes the game didn't work. And then we'd count cars. I'd be blue, Tommo'd be white, Teagan'd be red and Nan would be black. Sometimes we'd mix it up. The first one to get to ten won. Nan always won, no matter what colour she had. And she'd giggle wickedly and tell us better luck next time. She was funny, our nan. And she had so much grace. I miss her sometimes.

'So,' says Dildo quietly. 'Where are we gonna go now?'

Danny and Kyle share a look. Danny speaks. 'There's only one other guy round 'ere I know who'll take it but . . .'

'It'll be all right, mate,' Kyle smiles at him.

'Why?' says Danny, defensively. 'Have you dealt to him before?'

'Nah, mate. But they all started like us.' Kyle's face takes on that glazed film star look that is starting to bother me. He steps round Danny, lightly hugging his shoulder with the palm of his hand, and starts to walk down the road towards Langrick. 'Don't worry about it.' We watch his back, dithering, looking at the waves. 'Come on!'

Troy, Danny and Dildo look at me. 'Fuck it,' I sigh. 'Let's go.'

6

Riding in Cars with Boys

We head into the town centre, warily watching Kyle for sudden movements. We need a base to make plans, but like all things that happen in Clyde, it has to have that certain up-north pretty-crap make-do feel, so we opt for Danny's kitchen. Unfortunately we walk right in to where Davo, a twenty-eight-ish-year-old policeman, is sitting chatting up Danny's sister. The police here are part of the community – some square, some, off-duty, as corrupt as Fez. The best are somewhere in between. Since Kyle is in his film-star mode he decides to make something cinematic out of this chance meeting and nearly fucks things up for all of us. But first, we all pile in the kitchen, and freeze at the sight of Davo, with obligatory donut.

'Hello, lads,' he says. 'How do?'

We all look at each other.

'All right thanks, Davo,' we chime suspiciously. The atmosphere is tense. Davo and Danny's sister exchange looks and burst out laughing.

'You do look like twats in them glasses,' says Danny's sister.

'Oh, thanks a lot,' Danny flips her off and Kyle drags us all out and marches back round the front of the house.

'We have to get away now,' he hisses.

'What?' I look scornfully at him. I've perfected scorn. If Kyle's going to make a fucking film out of this, I'll be the hot, scornful one, I think.

'If Davo knows where we are, the moment he hears something is going down he'll be on us.' Kyle takes Danny's keys from his hands, opens the passenger door of his Citroën, and deftly throws the keys back to him. 'Danny – get in, we're driving.'

The rest of us exchange glances. 'Bloody hell,' Dildo grumbles.

We pile in, and Kyle actually says, 'Go, go, go.'

Jesus H. Christ.

Riding in cars with boys is not as fun as Drew Barrymore would have you believe. Riding in the back of Danny's car is terrifying, because I have *no* control. In this kind of situation you have to let go, and you do. You Let Go. Your life does not belong to you. You have entrusted it to the car itself, a runaround patch-up knocked together from quite a few other cars, half green and half purple, the brakes dodgy and the tyres cheap, and the driver an eighteen-year-old stoner who's pretending he's in *Snatch*. And as you realise this you wonder if you will ever get any again before you die, or if you're dead already and it's all just a blurry, beautiful dream. *Snatch*, I mean.

Halfway along the road from Osford to Langrick Danny's phone plays the tune from *Star Wars*. He picks it up, reads it and laughs. 'Oh, fuck.'

'What now?' I ask.

'I've just got a text from Davo. "I don't know what you're up to you with that tosspot Kyle, but if you come home now I'll let you off. Davo. PS. Your sister's fit."'

Danny grins at us ruefully, one hand on the wheel, one showing us the text. 'Maybe we better do this tomorrow.'

This is England.

7

Manchester or London or New Zealand

I'm doing exams at school Monday to Wednesday and Dildo has an STD check-up on Thursday, so we agree to meet on Friday night, when everyone is out on the town and we won't be so conspicuous. After arranging this, Dildo and I walk together from Langrick up to Osford while Kyle and Danny go for a pint, and I rant about life.

'I'm getting out. This is shit. I'm leaving and I'll have a long-distance thing with Rainbow, then I'll move to wherever she goes to uni. And win her back if everything is really fucked up. We had a fight about dealing. You want to get the fuck out of Dodge too, don't you?'

Dildo hesitates. 'Yeah.'

'You could come live with me, Dildo.' I cock my head to the side and look at him, grinning. 'We could start up a business. You can make loads of money on the internet right now. Or you could do an animation course and we'll start a cartoon series. We'll move to Manchester. Or London. Or New Zealand.'

There is a companionable silence as we walk. I can tell by the look on Dildo's face that he's dreaming.

'That would be cool.' Dildo gives me a hopeful smile. 'But I've got me mam to take care of. Her disabled benefits don't cover it all. And then there's my sister. Bex. Someone's got to be here to make sure she doesn't become a complete slapper.'

'True . . .' I laugh. 'Bit late, but true.'

'Yeah.' Dildo grins.

'We could do it,' I say, and we walk on a bit and reflect. We pass an old couple, out for a walk in shorts and hiking boots. I pet their dog and we call out hello then walk on.

'But Flick . . .' Dildo starts, then trails off.

'What?'

'Well . . .' He frowns. 'How?'

I turned my head towards him. 'How?'

'Yeah,' Dildo trudges on, watching his feet eat up the ground beneath them. 'Just seems to me . . . easier said than done.' He shrugs. 'I mean, how does anyone get out of here?'

Dildo's an oracle. Behind him the waves crash on the beach. He walks along, oblivious, kicking an empty Carling can. I look ahead to Osford, my home for fifteen years, me mam and dad's home for forty more, my grandparents' home before that. There is a silence.

I frown. 'Fucked if I know how.'

There's more silence. Dildo looks over at me. 'I'm sorry about Rainbow, Flick. I really liked her.'

I smile at him then watch the waves crash on the sand. 'Yeah . . . me too.'

I don't make it home. I get to my door, turn around and walk straight to Rainbow's.

I tell her I love her and that I'm sorry and that I don't want to talk about anything tonight, but could I just hold her? We kiss and we hug each other and she says she's sorry too. We don't talk about the argument or the deal, but we make dinner together and we watch reruns of *Friends* and curl up playing happy families, dreaming we're far away from reality and, with me cuddling her close, we go to sleep. Compared to Rainbow, getting out is just a consolation prize. But why can't we have both?

8

Hubris Part II

In the morning, Rainbow goes to college. Lucy drives her over there after giving us eggs on toast and I stay in her bedroom and nap for a bit longer after they've gone. I have an exam in the afternoon, so fuck whatever the school says, I'm not coming in 'til one.

I have a weird dream that makes me feel sick and angry when I wake up. Fez was fucking Rainbow. I get these dreams sometimes. Rainbow's had a lot of boyfriends. I haven't slept with anyone but Rainbow. And I've been feeling generally sick inside with all this shit going on, so maybe that's bred negativity inside my skull. My brain wanders back to our fight and I wonder again what she was talking about. Animals. Was the fight just a one-off? Or could she be going off me? Or am I just being a paranoid stoner?

I flick through her DVDs and watch three episodes of *Family Guy* back to back before the battery runs out on her laptop. Then I notice two packs of photos on top of her telly. I'm suddenly gripped by jealousy. Now, I don't know how this happens, how someone fairly logical can suddenly turn into a raving loony of mental patient proportions, but I just feel a switch flick over in me, and I look at the photos and I suddenly think, 'they'll be of her exes. There will be exes in them, and they will be naked and fucking.'

I walk over to the TV. I pick up the envelopes and I go through the photos expecting to find her exes, Daniel,

Raphael (her first), Jake, or Rainbow, naked, a cock in her mouth. Why do I do this to myself, I think as a pigtailed four-year-old Rainbow smiles excitedly back at me, all gappy-teeth and rosy cheeks, a proper family album photo. I find nothing, and start to feel a little guilty.

Ah well, it's only photos, she wouldn't mind me looking, says the little fucking persuasive devil on my shoulder.

I'm perusing the piles of paper on her desk. It's not a betrayal. I pull open the top drawer of a chest. A pack of cards, random crap, a note . . . I frown and unfold it . . . from . . . me. Sigh of relief. I pull open the second drawer. KY Jelly, condoms, an egg-shaped vibrator. Cream, pills, multivitamins, echinacea tablets. The bottom drawer of the three is electrical equipment, a mass of black wires with crumpled instructions in the middle. Nothing. Nothing at all. I am a sickly, masochistic detective, fervent in my quest to find the knowledge I seek.

I hear someone cross the landing and hope they didn't catch the noise of the drawers and think I was snooping. But of course they wouldn't. I'm above that. We are – me and Rainbow. She trusts me in her room – otherwise she wouldn't have left me here.

But then I notice a small file cabinet in the corner, covered in cushions and teddy bears. Rainbow calls me her teddy bear. There's a school bag and a stack of papers in front of it, which I carefully remove. I don't want to be doing this. My mind is slightly repulsed, but also a blank. My hands wander compulsively. My face in the mirror, my movements, remind me of Rainbow when she picks my spots. My face gets redder and redder and she apologises and draws back but her eyes lock on to another blocked pore and her fingers dive back in to squeeze out the puss. That's what I'm doing now. Squeezing out the puss.

There's a thick white envelope at the very back of all the files, crammed halfway down with other scraps of paper, birthday cards etc. There's a note from Jake that says 'Sorry! I'm a twat ☺ Friends?' on a picture of a cat. What a gay. Then there's a thick white envelope folded in four and ripped open. Inside is black writing on A4 lined notepaper. I reckon it at ten pages. It's twelve – helpfully and twattishly numbered. It starts 'Dear Rainbow'. I check the last page: 'Love Rafa'. I start to read it. 'We argued and teased each other, but we kissed that night on the beach and I felt you pressed against me and then we text later and you said you wanted to get to know me more.'

I shut the letter, put it back in the envelope, shove it in the cabinet and sit on the windowsill, sweating. It's exactly like she told me. Exactly. The voice of the better me in my head speaks: 'You have to trust her.' I look at her unmade bed and say aloud: 'I don't deserve you.' I'm on the windowsill for about ten minutes, thinking. Thinking it was a stupid thing to do and she doesn't need to know ANOTHER stupid thing I did. One of these times, something will change. She'll realise I'm weak and not good enough for her and that I don't respect her privacy like I should. It's ridiculous. I'm ridiculous. I only read a page and everything is just like she said so I'll stop. I'll stop with the letter and I'll stop with the whole subject of her exes. I've got het up about it before. I questioned her. I don't know why because it only fucks things up and makes her upset. The present Rainbow, my one, loves only me and that's all I need to know. Her past is really none of my business. My past isn't exactly without shadiness. If I read it, it will be exactly as she told me.

I wonder when he sent it. After the first time? Or the second, or the third? I jump off the windowsill, open the drawer and dive my hand back in like an addict reaching for a needle. I open it . . . 'I know after xmas you'll be in England . . .' Okay. After the second time. I let out a huge breath. All right, that's all I need to know. I flip back a few pages and start reading. 'I think about you all the time and want you to know that, if you want it to go on, I want it to go on. But I understand that you don't want this right now. I know you don't love me in quite the same way I love you.' Good . . . then I idly read the middle and my throat clogs up and my pits sweat so much I can feel it through my T-shirt. 'I know you were shy about admitting it but after that convo til four a.m. when we admitted how we felt we talked every night and I was so happy and so in love with you.' I put the letter down. My stomach knots up. She never told me that. Did she ever tell me that? She said it was never emotional on her part. I feel sick. Not with Rainbow, with myself. I'm so weak, I'm so shit, she is way too good for me. If she knew what I was really like she'd leave. I should walk out now, put a note on her bed telling her. She deserves someone better than me, stronger. A man. I am a fucking animal, with no self-control. I put my head in my hands and let out a sob. So fucking weak and stupid. I'm sitting thinking about it. Why am I reacting like this? There have been plenty of girls I've been like that with. She loves me. She'd tell me if she thought it mattered but to her it doesn't. She doesn't get jealous.

I wonder if Raphael's dick is bigger than mine. I wonder if Jake went down on her better than I do. I wonder why I never believe Rainbow when we talk about this shit. I need to re-read it. I've just read it quickly and I'm probably over-reacting. I screw up my face, take a deep breath and look at the letter, lying accusingly on the bed. It can't get any worse. I reread it, this time scanning the whole way through. It happens pretty much as Rainbow says, with extra emotion and horniness, though I suppose that could be in the interpretation of the writer. There are also some spelling mistakes that I'm sadistically pleased about. He, Raphael (fucking stupid name), says some things that make me think he doesn't know Rainbow as well as I do. Some obvious things that are really more surface-Rainbow, Rafa cites as Rainbow 'opening up'. The Rainbow in this dead reality eats from a McDonald's. My Rainbow would NEVER eat from a McDonald's. It's weird getting a stolen glimpse of a previous Rainbow. The things that bother me are:

1. Rafa says 'if you're ever in Madrid or you become a painter and can live here, we'll meet again'. Which makes me worry that she wanted to live with Rafa, 'cause that's a pretty big step, but also 'cause it's something we've talked about. So does Rainbow say this to everyone? Am I just one on the list?
2. The talking 'every night', I read forlornly. She hasn't told me about this. I imagine phone sex and feel shit.

I'm reading it to the end. The letter follows on from these conversations. It cites that Rafa knows it has to end and knows Rainbow doesn't love him, probably never will. I'm calming in relief. Only minimal shaking and sweating betray me now. The letter ends with much well wishing and love. I start to feel sorry for Rafa. He was probably a nice enough guy. And he loved my Rainbow, which I can definitely identify with. I'm the lucky one – Rafa would know that. And I'm risking it all for the sick self-indulgent pleasure of torturing myself. I fold the letter away quietly.

Rainbow, I think. I can't tell her right now because I can't lose her. I know I'm betraying her by keeping her when someone better could have her, but I love her. I love her and I'm so fucking ashamed of myself. I'm sorry Rainbow. I'm so sorry.

9

Doomsday

Friday night, pre-deal, I'm at Ash's place. I blasted through my exams – I couldn't say if I did well or not, but they're done – and stayed at Rainbow's again on the Thursday. She went to college early again, and I made sure I slept until she got back for lunch, after her morning classes, not running the risk of being conscious, knowing now how easily I can give in to temptation, knowing what a weak little shit I am. I may trust Rainbow. I don't trust myself.

So, it's Friday night, the arranged evening of the deal, and after a truly disturbing phone call from Kyle I'm already getting the sweats. Apparently we're going to some really weird, really serious crack house. Great. Kyle also said, 'Oh, yeah, and don't be seen doing anything crazy 'cause we could get banged up for years for this', which wasn't very helpful on the whole staying-calm front. Meanwhile I'm starting to think maybe we should just sell it off in parts so we're not dealing with anyone properly mental, and this conundrum has left me at a loss for what to do – whether to meet the boys tonight, or to bunk off and convince them to do it an-other time, in smaller cuts. Ash has filled in the others on my situation after a particularly long phone call in which I explained to her every which way I am fucked (vis à vis the deal – I don't tell anyone about my OCD at Rainbow's). She flicked through a magazine (I could hear the pages turning) and every so often gave an infuriating, 'yeah', so I'm still impatiently awaiting advice. From anyone. When I get there I brief Mike on it as we go up the stairs, but inside the attention is firmly on other matters so I wait for my turn to rant. I pace the flat with a fixed frown and chain-smoke maniacally. Daisy and Trix are there, and the girls are looking at Trix's portfolio of modelling shots she had done last week at Sandford shopping centre that her pervy old boyfriend paid for. This is entertainment (and that was deadpan sarcasm). They chat about girly shit and I can *feel* the clock ticking on the mantelpiece.

'Wow, they've done a great job on your hair, haven't they?' Ash.

'D'you think I should get some done?' Ella.

'Definitely, I am, we should all go!' Daisy.

'I'm going to put them on myspace and see how many comments I get! Heeheehee!!' Trix. What kind of stupid fucking twatty name is Trixie. I can feel my blood boiling. The clock chimes eight.

'Ooo, wow, your highlights look pretty!'

'Jesus,' I mutter.

Fucking hell. Fucking hell. Fucking hell.

'Look, Flick, don't she look great?'

'Yeah.' I swig some water. 'Airbrushing is a beautiful thing, now can we get to my problems, please?'

'Huh?' Trixie says, staring at the photos, wondering what airbrushing is.

'What's so wrong with this that it's such a crime to you, Flick?' Ash rolls her eyes at me.

'Nothing, nothing at all, it's just a massive stereotype and utterly pointless, vain, boring and pathetic.' I mimic Trix to perfection: '"I'm going to be a model and a WAG because basically I have no GCSEs and no other choice." It's a beautiful, beautiful thing and I'm glad your lives are so full, but you'll all get knocked up next year anyway so it doesn't matter right now! Can we move on to something important, like how I'm going to do this deal and get out of this shithole without getting killed by Fez?'

'FUCK, Flick!' A sudden, and completely unexpected, outburst from Ashley. She stands up to her full height, which is actually quite impressive when you include her hair. 'No we can't!' She glares at me like I'm the Antichrist, there is a stony silence, and when I start to speak again she cuts in angrily. 'I'm fucking fed up of you coming round here looking down on us all as if you're fucking *deigning* to spend time with us and refusing to fuck us as if we're *beneath* you.'

'What the fuck—' I say, outraged, but she cuts me off, waving her WKD Blue in the air.

'You don't want to be a stereotype, Flick, but you play your own games to replace the ones you avoid and you fill a role and a place in the grand scheme of things, just like everyone else does. I'm sick and fucking tired of you thinking you're better than us. You might not be a slag, Flick, and you might not treat women like shit, but you're a stoner and a druggie and a cock when you're drunk and you throw up everywhere just like the rest of us so fuck you, Will Flicker.'

She gestures at Daisy, Ella and Trix, both sitting on the crummy sofa trying not to look at me but unable to take their eyes off us, me and Ash, facing each other down like bulls.

'At least Trix is trying to make a go of it. What are you doing with your life, eh? Pissing and whining over a deal. If you weren't a coward, you'd tell Fez no and take the beating. But you won't and not 'cause there's no way out, but because without the fucking drama of this fucking deal there's nothing really in your life, Flick. You FUCKING WASTER.' Ash pounds the floor across the flat, and, with her last words, exits into the bathroom. She slams the door and we hear sounds of her rolling a joint and bursting out crying. I leap over to the door, kicking bottles out my way, and yell through it.

'Ashley! ASHLEY! You FUCKING open this door!' All the heat and muscle that there is in my body feels fucking angry, like a fire that's been poked into life, the coals turned over 'til the flames lick up through the chimney. I beat on the door with a fist. 'FUCKING OPEN IT!'

'FUCK OFF!' She screams, choking on something – tears, smoke, pills, who the fuck knows.

'WILL!' A deep voice yells from behind me. I turn around, staring at the group, Trix, Daisy, Ella, Josh, Jamie and Mike, dotted over the living room. I stare wildly at the three guys.

'What?' I spit murderously from between curled lips. Silence. I measure in at about six foot, same as the other guys, but I'm broader than most of my friends. I look older than them, my shoulders and frame wider than most, in a good way. I'm muscular, my eyes are so dark they're almost black, and my face is meaner and rougher looking. I look like your stereotypical fucking rough 'un, narrow-eyed and old before his time. Maybe I'm soft underneath, but you wouldn't try it to see. At least, Josh, Jamie and Mike don't. No one says anything.

Ashley screams again from the bathroom, in between scarcely disguised sobs: 'FUCK OFF!'

I punch the door one last time, flinging my right arm carelessly at the wood.

'Upset 'cause I wouldn't fuck you, Ash?' She bursts out with fresh tears and I shake my head and articulate disgust to the ceiling: 'Fucking slag.'

I walk over to where Ash's wallet is and spitefully, half

unaware of what I'm doing, take out a small handful of notes. Josh moves as if to stop me and I stare coldly into his eyes. His hand falters mid-air and drops back to his side. He looks down, eyes flickering away from my own. It's at this point that I have more power over any of my mates in the room, and, ironically, the least over myself. I have lost it. I am taking thirty quid from a friend for no reason whatsoever, other than to get her back for being a bitch. I'm not even sure if she was being a bitch. Sentences from her outburst start to make sense, and I block them out of my head by frowning, the simplicity of me being right and Ashley being wrong that much easier to deal with than the reverse. I nod at Josh, narrowing my eyes for just a second.

'That's right.' I feel like I'm watching myself from above, as if I'm a character in a film. The mean one, the one that gets shot towards the end. Shit, I think abstractedly, I hope I don't get shot. Then, 'Nah, you won't, you've thought of it now.' I walk out of the apartment to silence from the main room and, in the background as if on a loop, Ash shouting 'FUCK YOU, FLICK, FUCK YOU!' Extremely cinematic, I think. I call Kyle and he meets me with Dildo and Danny in the square.

IO

Scum

'Fucking bitch deserves all she gets,' is Kyle's evaluation of the Ashley situation. Kyle seems to have become a meaner fucker in days. He stands head stuck out, hands on hips as if ready for battle, and his speech flows between serious *Snatch*-style thug and a complete parody of the same character.

We're standing in a dim fucking alleyway, shit all about us. Danny kicks a takeaway carton away from him. The windows of the flat in front of us are boarded up and, according to Kyle, a clapped-out fucking junkie lives inside. We're going to try and sell him the coke. I'm not exactly looking forward to it. But I think, fuck it, if a twathead like Fez can make a deal so can I. I can be fucking scary too. I can be the big cock in the room, as the incident at Ash's proved. I light up a joint and we pass it about.

Kyle taps out a code on the door, but it swings open, already unlocked.

'OI!' he shouts. 'Anyone in?'

We hear a moan in the back and kick our way through bits of old cardboard boxes and newspaper to a dingy living room. The whole place reeks of piss. We hear coughing coming from the stairs, and a lanky guy, with limp brown hair, wearing a vest and grey cord trousers practically falls into the room with us. He looks familiar but I can't place from where. We move closer in the dingy light. This is when I notice his veins. They stick out on his pale yellow skin like someone has drawn them in blue biro down his arms. There is a massive bruise on the inside of each elbow, golden-brown underneath, with fresh blue-purple rings in the centre. Worse than these fresh track marks are scars, where his skin makes tiny whorls, like burst blisters in a row on his forearm. The veins protrude, so these little marks are thrust at us. He stares at us, confused, zombified. He looks sweaty, which is probably the most trivial thing I could note right now.

We all look to Kyle, who has gone suddenly quiet. Fucking hell. Wimp. I shake my head, push past him and walk forward decisively.

'We have some coke to sell,' I say. 'You want in?'

The zombie looks at us. 'How much you got?'

I shrug, and because in reality I have no idea I simply pull the package out of Kyle's hands and show him. 'That much.'

The zombie leans forward like an inquisitive bird, his eyes lighting up. I'm reminded of kids on their birthdays. 'That's a lot.' He looks back at us. We exchange glances and wait for something a little more concrete. 'I think I'll have to ask Mark.' He turns around unsteadily and, holding the banister, stumbles back up the stairs. We hear a muted conversation.

Danny looks at me incredulously and mouths, 'Mark? Oo, how posh!'

'Come on up!' A deeper voice, not the zombie's, shouts us from above. We climb the stairs. The stairwell is tiny and we have to go one by one. No one wants to go first, so I do. At the top of the stairs there are three doors. A green light emanates from one of them.

I retch as soon as I'm through the door. The room reeks of BO and piss. A skinny blonde girl, with the same lank hair as Zombie, who I swear to god cannot be older than thirteen, lies naked, except for a pair of dirty grey knickers and square, black sunglasses, on a large bean bag. She has abscesses all over her body, and her nose is bleeding. An older guy steps off of her and zips up his fly. This is Mark.

'How do, lads?' He pulls on a T-shirt that says 'Monkey See Monkey Do' in yellow letters on blue. He looks about twenty-nine and in slightly better shape than the others. Still, he doesn't have any meat on his bones. His face is ratty, his nose pointy and eyes dark and hooded. He looks like Josh Hartnett on smack. To be fair, he's weirdly attractive.

He grins. 'Heard you've got something for me?'

I hear Danny whisper behind me, 'Just do it and let's get out.' So I watch my hand pull the packet out of my jacket. Mark darts in towards me and takes it instantly.

'Who mashed it up?' He holds it up to the light.

'I don't know.' I frown, trying not to show on my face that I don't know what 'mashed it up' means. 'Fezzer?'

'Fez? He's a dick.' Mark chuckles darkly. I get the feeling we could be friends if it weren't for the fact that Mark's supposed to be the most fucked up guy this side of Sandford. 'It doesn't look quality.' He tosses it back to us. 'I'll give you Seven Fifty.'

'Bollocks!' Luckily Kyle pipes up. 'I cut it myself. It's good shit. There's eight eight-balls there. Twelve hundred quid for the lot.'

'What the fuck am I going to do with this much coke, eh?' Mark suddenly gets aggressive. 'I hope you little shits aren't wasting my time.'

'Don't call me a little shit,' says Dildo, slowly and hesitantly. He stands a foot above Mark.

'All right, mate,' Mark grins, suddenly overly friendly again. 'Just a question, did you know you can get life for dealing?'

'No, you can't,' says Kyle. 'You can get fourteen years but not life.'

'Erm, no.' Mark laughs and then his face drops. 'You can get life.' We are suddenly all nervous. We look at each other. Mark bursts out with what I can only describe as a guffaw. 'Didn't you know that? Fucking hell!' He makes a noise like he's choking, wheezing, having an asthma attack or something and I'm in half a mind to make him sit down and put his head in between his legs, but then the wheezing slows and he stand upright and pats his chest. 'I'll tell you what . . .'

The blonde girl spits up behind him. Seriously. It happened. This occurs on my periphery as my pupils are rooted to Mark, this oddly charismatic bundle of energy in the middle of the room.

'I'll tell you what. I'll take three-quarters of it then, for nine hundred pound, all right?' Everyone looks at me. Kyle shrugs.

'All right,' I say quietly.

'All right!' Mark jovially scoops the coke back from me and weighs it on some scales, overlooked by Kyle and myself. He gives us the leftovers in the bag, along with the cash, wrapped up in a paper bag, looking like lunch, and grins at us. 'See? I've more than halved your troubles. Aren't we mates now?'

Zombie stands up in the background and gets a beer out of a small Coca-Cola fridge. I knew not to trust Coca-Cola. He leans against Mark, who puts his arm round poor Zombie, licks a finger and sticks it in the coke. He smiles widely. 'I like it.'

We turn to go. 'Thanks, Mark,' I say.

As I get to the door – first in, last to leave, I feel a rough hand on my shoulder.

'Hey,' Mark's big dark pupils ask me innocently, almost pleading with me. 'Aren't we mates now, yeah?'

We hold eyes for a moment. I try to work out whether he's serious. He looks almost concerned. Poor bastard. He's as fucked as Fez and maybe more. I wonder if the real Mark is just a shadow to him now, someone that used to exist before he bought his emotions off some scummy dealer. I pat him on the arm.

'Yeah, Mark, we're mates,' I nod sincerely.

As I follow Dildo's silhouetted frame out the front door I finally realise where I know Zombie from: he was two years above me in school, the blonde girl on the bean bag his younger sister.

II

How Not to Climax

We're suddenly all fucked. Not literally (I wish) but we're fucked as in all the energy goes out of us. I realise that in Mark's place I was still as a rock but now, outside in the cold and the dark, my shoulders are going like a pneumatic drill (i.e. shaking violently). We're walking away from the house and it seems we all decide at the same time to start laughing.

'FUCK!' shouts Danny. 'That was FUCKING ridiculous! Did you see that slapper?'

'She was OFF her FU-cking tits, mate, and what the fuck was with Mark? What kind of name is fuckin' MARK for a dealer?' Kyle snorts.

Dildo joins in to be companionable. 'The guy we saw first looked like something out of *Shaun of the Dead.*'

Kyle passes round the bag and we all wet our fingers, dip them in, and lick up the blow like sherbet. I just laugh along, really loudly. We all do, and we don't stop. None of us want to stop.

We end up at Fez's, whether by accident or design I'll never know, and Kyle busts into Fez's bedroom, interrupting him having another go at Hannah and throws the cash down. He is followed closely by Danny who holds the bag.

'There you go, we got your nine hundred, and the packet's worth another three. You've made a hundred. Job done.'

Danny nods in agreement, meaning that's your lot, Fez.

'Two hundred!' I yell from the landing.

'Sorry – two hundred. Flick, come in you tossbag,' says Kyle's voice. I enter. Fez looks totally out of it. Kyle is saying, 'Look, I can do some other deals for you. How about we take it to Sandford—'

'Nah,' Fez waves at him, half-conscious. 'No fucking way, police are all over it. That's good – ' he nods to the blow. 'I'll do that, and take the money. I'm thinking of lending Hannah out for cash anyway.'

Hannah hits him and laughs. She sounds like Janice from *Friends* and we all, including Fez, visibly recoil.

'But, but I can do more!' Kyle looks put out. His days as a movie-star-cum-coke-dealer cut short before they had truly begun. Me and Danny roll our eyes at each other. Fez does the same to himself.

'Enough. Me and Hannah'll try the first line, why don't you guys make yourself comfortable downstairs and I'll chuck you down the bag when we're done?'

Well, well. We've made it into the Fez inner circle. Danny and I are now raising eyebrows at each other.

'All right then,' Danny says and we turn for the door while Kyle stands dejected in the middle of the room. 'Come on, Kyle. I think I saw a PlayStation in't living room, you can deal to hos and black guys on *Taxi Driver*.'

I snort and we leap the stairs downwards.

PART FIVE

I

In for a Penny

'FUCKING NOTHING HAPPENS AROUND HERE.'

It's an hour later and the five of us are sitting about feeling pissed off round Fez's, still waiting for him and Hannah to finish the 'first go', when Kyle lets out a frustrated shout and slams his open palm into the banister.

We all look up at him from our various slouched positions and I murmur, 'That's very insightful of you, Kyle.'

'Fucking *nothing*. Fucking nothing ever happens.' Kyle throws his cigarette out the open door and gestures to us with a shrug of his shoulder. We head up the stairs to Fez's room, his hallowed space in this three-bed semi that he shares with Tylo, another dealer, and a blonde university graduate called Lara, who left for Leeds five years ago, came back with a degree in English and Music and has done nothing since but get stoned, work at Morrisons and talk about her band, which none of us have ever heard play. Rock on, Lara.

Kyle walks into Fez's room first, banging the door open. It promptly falls off the hinges. 'What the fuck is this? We've been waiting an hour!'

'Hey!' Fez stands up angrily. Hannah is sprawled on the bed, sniffing and wiping her nostrils. Fez stares at us, stoned, pissed, coked out of his mind. 'Hey,' he says again. Then he neatly passes out, falling back onto the bed.

Kyle takes the bag of blow off a pile of underwear by the foot of the bed. He looks at me. I look at myself in the mirror. I've been smoking steadily for an hour and am perhaps more stoned now than I've ever been. Kyle shakes the little clear plastic bag at me. I giggle, shrug, and he saunters up to me, all happy, and lands a smacker on my cheek. Ah, well. In for a penny, in for a pound.

2

Ramblings of a Coked-up Critic

'It's like how all these social commentary films have the anti-hero dying at the end. Because the message is that failure and self-destruction are not sustainable. But who d'you think pays taxes on these like, luxury goods designed to distract us from our lives or make 'em better, who works in the factories that make our economy so amazing, who buys into all that shit? The common man, on a downward spiral from bliss and innocence to degradation and poverty – us, that's who – me and you, Flick! Because genius is a temporary state; bright sparks burn out; bitter experience deadens hope for improvement. *Failure*, self-destruction is the only thing that is truly sustainable, Flick. That's why *Trainspotting* was so brilliant. The anti-hero, the fucking lanky junkie, prevails. Whether he takes drugs again or not is irrelevant. He's still a fuck-up.' Kyle says all this lying on his back with a joint in one hand and a coke-lined Clyde County library card in the other. I sniff over the coffee table and white powder flies up my nose, making it tingle so hard I poke it to see if it's okay.

'It feels like it's melting.'

'Oh, don't worry about that mate, it's not.' Kyle waves smoke at me dismissively.

I wipe my nostrils self-consciously. 'So what references would you cite for that opinion?'

'References?'

'Don't tell me you've forgotten everything you learnt in

English literature *already*, Kyle Craig.' I parody our Scottish Eng. lit. teacher, Ms Clarkson, to perfection and Kyle snorts a laugh, fine white dust escaping his nostrils.

'Oh aye, laddie, well, I would have to cite Irvine Welsh's essay on the inside cover of the Orange edition of *Trainspotting*, erm . . .'

'Only *one* reference! You'll have to do better than *that*, Mr Craig, or it's a *D* fer *you*!'

'All right, hang on! Err . . . also *Fight Club*, for the "masturbation is" speech, George Orwell's *1984* speech about the need for a continuing state of war . . . and Michael Moore's *Fahrenheit 9/11* for introducing me to said speech.'

'The former or the latter of the two aforementioned speeches?'

'Oh, the latter, Ms Clarkson.'

'Why thank you, Kyle.'

3

What Is Love?

I get a text from Rainbow halfway through our little pile of joy and in my excited bleariness, I decide to call her, stumble into the hallway and slump on the doorstep, pressing my mobile to my ear. As the phone begins to ring, I suddenly remember my paranoid invasion of her privacy, the revelation of the circumstances of her adoption and how I acted, the way she looked at me when I ate those space cakes, and the fact that I'm wrist-deep in blow. The animal thing, the screaming, the comparison to her parents didn't mean a thing. She was just frightened and upset and I was the one who had frightened and upset her. She didn't want to lose me and was throwing everything she had at it. I see it clearly now, I think, and then it suddenly blurs into a haze again and all I'm left with is the feeling that my heart is sinking to my gut and my knowledge that I was and am totally in the wrong, and Rainbow is the pinnacle of everything that's right in the world. Shit. I feel hollow, sick and panicked. The coke seems to be acting like a truth serum. I can't lie to her, I think, feeling my heartbeat in my throat.

'Hello? . . . Hello?'

I swallow and my lips tremble. 'Hi, Rainbow.'

'Hello, sweetheart!'

I'm a bastard. I'm a bastard. I'm a big sodding twat . . . I'm a cocked-up coke . . . no . . . coked-up cock bastard. And she's going to leave me. She's going to leave me here alone without Rainbow in my life. I love her so much. 'I love you so much.' I say. And then suddenly everything blurs again and my mind changes, like switching from Jekyll to Hyde.

'I love you too.'

She doesn't know it, the voice says – back again but this time it's a queer tinny twisted voice – but she's saying that to me with coke everywhere around the room.

Everything is fucking up. Everything is fucking up at the same time, and I feel myself falling down a long black tunnel (like Alice through the rabbit-hole, says the voice) and somehow . . . without the inclination to make myself stop . . . It's weird but this falling feels good, it feels good to be knowing that it will end, even if it will end badly and everything will fuck up, because at least that knowledge is definite. They say if you never try you'll never know, but I think as well if you try you'll never know how things are going to turn out, and I don't want to never know. The uncertainty kills me. Wasn't it all just simpler, I hear in a tinny rant, when there was nothing to look forward to, no future with Rainbow to protect? When we knew where we would live and who we would know forever? Don't you just want to give up on making this huge effort to get out and change things? Change isn't necessarily for the better. Life's all right, isn't it? You're not an African baby with flies on your face.

Stupid racist voice, I say. It seems my brain is not my brain entirely at the moment. It is running on coke and smoke and JD and the other kind of Coke and, more importantly, the massive release of pain-numbing adrenalin you get when everything is fucking up at the same time.

—I'm ready for this to fuck up, it says. Don't worry, I can deal, I'm *prepped*. She's gonna leave you and we're gonna move on. No fucking problem.

—Fuck. Fuck. Fuck. Rainbow. I love you.

—Huh! My brain exclaims. What is love? A firing of synapses in your head! A chemical surge! Two people gazing stupidly at each other! Whatever. It's not specific to this one girl. There will always be someone else. Yeah, it could be Rainbow, but it could be anybody. You don't need *Rainbow*. What kind of fucking stupid name is Rainbow?

—Rainbow . . . Rainbow . . . fuck . . . fuuuuck . . .

The thing about other people leaving you, is that it's cathartic, especially if you part on bad terms. You cut them off, you don't see them, you don't need to hurt at all. You can go dead inside, and the simplicity of this feels amazing. Maybe as well, it's a self-fulfilling prophecy: you always think you'll be dumped and when you are, it's satisfying to know you were right. You were right about the world – it *is* a load of shit, she *was* just a bitch who would eventually stop caring about you! Good for *you*, brother! The problem is that, right now, I'm so high I want that cathartic simplicity, honesty, to get it all out and have my sins absolved. So my brain is thinking, fuck it – better to have her dump me over the letter than dump me over the mound of white stuff I've just snorted.

Am I thinking clearly? I think to me, to myself, to my own brain. Which is strangely throbbing, though not in a painful way. I can't lie to her. I never did deserve her. You're a fucking waster, Flick, my head says. You're not on her level, she's out of your league. She always was. I swallow. I leave a pause. My pulse beats loudly in my right cranium.

'Flick?'

'Fuck.'

4

Punishing Consciousness

I tell Rainbow about reading the letter. She doesn't shout or scream or want to hit me or leave me. She sounds more pissed off at me than I've ever known her to be, now that I've done this coupled with the fight the other day, but she still doesn't sound very pissed off. She says she's angry but she understands. She kept the letter because it was deeply felt by the person who wrote it and she didn't have the heart to throw it away. She has no feelings for Raphael, or any of her exes. They didn't speak every night, and Rainbow doesn't remember any big conversation.

'Sometimes people see things how they want to see them,' Rainbow tells me quietly. No, they didn't have phone sex, they only spoke on msn. Rainbow talked to a lot of people on msn, do I want their names and backgrounds too? The fact that I didn't trust her or respect her privacy makes her angry, not particularly the fact that I read the letter. She sometimes wants to snoop around my place, or read my texts. No, she hasn't. I'm not a twat, it's okay. I do deserve her: 'Stop saying that, Flick.' I tell her that I'm sorry about her adoption, that I'm going to stop using, that the deal is over and that everything is over and that I hope she will be able to forgive me and that I'll do anything to make it up to her, because she is my best friend and she's beautiful inside and out and because she means more to me than anything in the world. It feels like we're saying goodbye.

'I wish you were here,' she says sadly. 'I wish I could hug you.' We talk for twenty minutes and then she has to go and pick up Tim from his friend's house. Her mums don't like him walking back alone. She thinks I've been drinking, and tells me to stop. And that she loves me. I feel like the most worthless piece of dirty, disgusting shit in the whole fucking world.

I hang up miserably and plod through to rejoin Danny, Dildo and Kyle, who hands me back the straw sympathetically. I look at Kyle. He blows me a kiss. I am so depressed I could kill everyone else. I lean forward, wishing I could be unconscious, wishing I was dead, wishing I could snort my whole fucking existence away. I watch Danny KO Dildo on *Tekken*.

I want to float into insignificance, I think in a dull, matter of fact way. I want to embrace the dark black hole. Be it K hole or coke hole. At this moment I am willing to take anything to make everything go away. Scratch that. To make me go away from everything else, so I can stop tainting it and turning pure things into shitty, hollow, lifeless wrecks. There is no point in being present. Consciousness hurts like a physical wound. I am a bad person. I am hurting the person I love the most, a person who is blameless and vulnerable and honest and who tries to be good, not in a pious way but in a soulful, kind, caring way. A person who has already been hurt enough, who was unloved and let down and discarded by the people that were supposed to care for her the most and I'm doing it to her again. And I'm lying to her about it. Ergo, it would be better if I was not here, and she could move on with her life. Oh, take me, self-pity, drag me down into your sweet nothingness. I imagine a high like a Galaxy advert – sweet, smooth . . . chocolatey. Come on, I think impatiently, sucking up another line, and then taking a toke of pot, then necking a pill Kyle proffers. Come on, take me the fuck away. FUCK! Even this fucking shit isn't working. I do another line. Fuck. Fuck. Fuck. Fuck. Fuck Rainbow, fuck me, fuck Montauk, fuck animation, fuck it all, because this is starting to feel good. Weird tingly, orgasmic good, with a sort of side dish of melting, fizzing that feels like the kind of good that's bad for you, the kind of good that has a lot of calories. I'm on the slide, the slide into being not here. Come on you beauty, I think. Drown me in this black sea of blow. I laugh suddenly. With glee I realise I'm going to black out. I know, because I always think like a right poet slash twat when I'm on the way under. And then I see the light very brightly and it sends some sort of shooting feeling through my skull. I feel panicked, and at the same time, utterly calm.

Kyle lights up a smoke. 'The thing about Almodovar, is that his earlier films were—'

'SHUT THE FUCK UP, KYLE.'

'What?'

I open my mouth wide, with no knowledge of what is to come out, and find myself screaming. 'CRITICISM IS NEVER AS VALUABLE AS CREATIVITY.'

And with that, as my legs give way beneath me, I get my wish – unconsciousness.

5

My Head, My Head

It's a little later. I think I've been half asleep, and I'm woken up by a huge pulse in my head. Kyle is still talking, unencumbered by my outburst.

'The problem is that everything we own costs money. And you have to have it just to keep up.'

I stand up slowly. The left side of the room is lower than the right.

'And then you have to buy property in a fucking good location, just to keep all this stuff safe.' Kyle is emphasising every word and each one beats like a hammer on the inside of my skull.

'We don't need all this shit, man! We can be free! Free, like that dude Martin in *Amores Perros*!'

Oh god. My head. My head. My head.

I hear the front door open and close. Then, suddenly, Gav appears, blurred and haloed in my vision by an ethereal light – dreamlike – and scampers up to me with his grin, his huge grin that I'm suddenly terrified by. It looks like he's going to fucking *eat* me.

'All right, our Flick?' His voice is sped up, high like he's sucked down helium. He seems to be moving really fast, jumping up and down, gesturing, shaking. Or perhaps it's the outline of his body. Perhaps it's moving so fast the particles are heating up and he's turning from a solid into a liquid.

'Gav,' I whisper, grabbing him, scared for him, trying to warn him. 'You're melting.' I hear his voice calling me from a distance, echoing, the sound of his words retreating, as if space were being stretched out. 'Don't move,' I say. 'You'll be okay if you don't move.'

Gav leans down the tunnel between us. His twitchy eyes flick back and forth, looking into mine searchingly. One giant vibrating hand comes closer to me, the edge wiggling like those little lines that float across your pupils in the fluid in your eye. Maybe time is being stretched out too and I'm seeing how things really are before the eye processes them, like seeing the movements between the twenty-five frames of film per second in one of Kyle's foreign movies.

'Flick?' Gav, so far away, touches my arm. 'Flick? Are you okay?'

6

Riding in Cars with Boys Part II

We're going through the centre of town. I'm looking down, but I can tell where we are because the bridge makes my tummy jump up and land in a horrible slow roll and I taste sick at the back of my throat.

'Look at that little piece of pussy.'

'Fez, keep your eyes on the road!'

'What?' I say. It's like I am present but everyone else is very distant from me, down a long dark corridor. I am aware of Fez's hostile presence in the car and I am frightened. But it seems that Gav is also here. I can hear him talking in my ear. Gav, the voice of reason.

I grin. It's a desperate fucking situation when Gav is the voice of reason. Suddenly a pain flashes through my skull, my head falls forward like a dead weight and for a second I black out again.

'Woh! Woh, woh, it's okay, man, it's nothing, you just concentrate on me, okay? It's gonna be okay, it's me, it's Gav, you'll be fine, man, you'll be fine.' Gav's eyes are wide and his bottom lip gets caught on his top one. 'You'll be fine.'

I've never seen him like this. I look up to the windscreen and watch the car straight-line a corner. Headlights strike us full in the face and the oncoming car's horn wails in protest. Fez swerves round it without a movement of his stony psycho face. I see those twitchy blue eyes in the mirror fixed hard on the road. I hear the rev count go up as we hit the straight towards the hospital. He's completely coked up. And he's enjoying this. The bastard. My brain starts to feel like it's pressing on the inside of my skull. I let out a small noise from between my teeth, which are bit around my tongue. Something starts to hurt and I can't tell where, and suddenly all I can think about is: Rainbow.

7

White Room

Gav must have walked me through the corridor and put my head gently on the desk while he spoke to the receptionist, because it's the kind of thing Gav would do in a crisis. Gav was soft in the head from all the pot, yes, but on the plus side it made him a puppy to all those he considered his friends. He must have done this, but I was twitching like a psychiatric case and to me it felt like I had been dragged through the waiting room by some beefy bodyguard whose hands pinched bruises into my arms and who kept taking quick digs into my spine with his knee. When we got to the counter my head smacked into it, my nose definitely broken, and I was sure blood was pouring out of me onto the white counter-top, like Edward Norton when his head gets fucked up under the bar in *Fight Club*. I groan.

Somewhere in the distance, like an echo from down a long corridor, I hear Gav's voice. 'What floor should I . . .? I don't know amounts . . .'

'. . . more specific . . .'

'. . . Quite a lot? I dunno, I wasn't there . . .'

'. . . who was with . . .'

'. . . his mates . . . young . . . didn't know what to do . . .'

'. . . illegal substances . . . toxic?'

'. . . not sure what . . . not exactly ibuprofen . . .'

'. . . age . . . national insurance numbercard . . .'

'*What?*'

Some time must have passed because, although I'm not aware of having moved anywhere, I'm now sitting on a doctor's bed, encircled by blue curtains, flanked by Dildo and Gav, who is now answering different questions.

'He keeps going . . . a bit, a bit blurry like he can't see and shaking and he was sick a lot and he keeps holding his head and saying Rainbow.'

Rainbow.

'Like that.'

'Rainbow! She's a girl!'

The doctor looks up from his notepad. 'Rainbow's a girl?'

'Yes, she's a girl,' I murmur into Dildo's jacket.

I can't make out his face but the doctor's head tilts to look at Gav. Gav shakes his head. A chasm opens in front of me – I'm on top of the steelworks and falling, my tummy, my spleen, my colon, my balls, my dick, my legs, my heart, my lungs drop into my head. My eyes roll up, I feel myself simultaneously retching and leaning backward, everything fades to black, and just before I lose consciousness I hear Gav say: 'There ain't a girl called Rainbow.'

8

An Arc of Coloured Light in the Sky Caused by the Rain's Refraction of the Sun's Rays

There are some things that are too painful to say in the first person. I see myself from the outside and the realisation of where I've ended up is sick, stuck in my throat. I see myself clearly, objectively, as Rainbow might see me.

Of course, there is a girl called Rainbow. In my fucked-up state, I was gripped with fear that maybe I'd made her up, and didn't think about the more logical explanation: that Gav had been doing community service all summer and had never met her. Four months had gone by since that night, my entire life had changed, and to a friend in the same town there hadn't even been a ripple in the water.

She visits me in the hospital. Rainbow, I mean. I open my eyes from a sleep, and she's stood at the door. She's ethereal, a dream. She was a really beautiful dream, I think. And I start crying.

And she starts crying. The light from the window hits exactly where she stands in the doorway, making her fluff of hair look like a lion's mane, a frieze of fire circling her heart-shaped face. She wears a white slip of a dress with a dark leather band around her right upper arm, and dirty white trainers falling off her feet. Her eyes are electric and blue and open wide in worry. She'll never have to worry like that again. Maybe at another time it would have worked out. But everyone has to climb a rocky path before reaching that rainbow. And me, I was just learning how to climb, fucking up, making mistakes.

She was a rainbow. A sign of hope proved illusory. An arc of coloured light in the sky caused by the rain's refraction of the sun's rays. I wasn't ready to be in her spotlight.

The thing about Rainbow was that she knew the truth in people. You met her eyes, you were illuminated in her light, and devastated, because you saw that she knew you, right through, every flaw. She branded you with her rays. I couldn't stay there. The pressure was intense. My complexion wrecked. I couldn't keep it up.

So I lost someone that had meant the world to me. Only I guess I didn't realise it, just then.

9

A Poem

I read this book once, maybe it was for class, maybe at Rainbow's, I can't remember. It was a collection of poems by this guy Corey Elwood Dean. One read:

> I make these choices
> I don't know where they will lead
> Before
> But after
> The devastation on your face
> Disappointment
> Again
> The first time was the worst
> Flashes of colour desaturated
> The ones later meant less.

I bet you anything he was talking about a girl.

IO

Loose Ends

You thought that was the end? It would probably have been way better if it was, all Hollywood and devastation and that. But life's not all bad! Although the following doesn't really lend any weight to that claim. Anyway. There's one more piece to the story.

Just before the summer ends I'm in Sandford city centre of a late afternoon. It's a Saturday, a lot of people are out, walking up and down the high street and buying things in the summer sales. I'm shopping on my own, walking towards the station, about to catch the train back. In one of my assorted carrier bags there is a bracelet in red, yellow, green, blue, orange, and pink chunky beads that I've bought for Ash, to make up with her. There is also a DVD, a book on flash animation, a bib for Teagan's baby, and a white short-sleeved T-shirt. I turn a corner and finish texting (unfortunately not Rainbow – in fact, me mam), press send and look up to a shout.

'Fucking little cocksucker.' Fez.

Fez in full flow, shirt open and spitting in Kyle's face.

'You owe it me, Fez. You're a piece of shit,' Kyle is saying.

Danny stands behind Kyle, his big form proud, his fists clenched. Troy is behind Fez, more nervous. Around them stand about ten of my friends, scattered between the two forming groups. I look for Ash. She isn't there. I watch what unfolds as if from in front of a television screen, or behind a wall of glass.

'FUCK you.' Fez grabs Kyle's shirt. 'If you think—'

But Kyle has seen this coming. He pulls Fez towards him and swings him around to his right side. The unexpected momentum has Fez on the floor. Kyle kicks his face and Fez pulls him down by the leg and pushes himself up off of Kyle's body. He takes three steps back and returns, like a wave on the shore, with force. Gav isn't there, but Troy, Limbo and another lad I don't know join Fez, quick-stepping forward, leaning on their back feet and jabbing fists into their opponents' faces, like synchronised dancers. Kyle and Danny take the punches and add more of their own. Dildo, stood at the back of the crowd, hesitant, awkward, my gentle giant, sees the inequality in the size of the groups and heads forward reluctantly to rectify the situation. He pushes Fez off Kyle. Fez stumbles backward and I watch Kyle's hand pull something out of his pocket and shake it downwards. He steps forward again and a girl in a black dress and pink shoes screams. Danny's girl.

This doesn't make me proud. I don't know what I should have done. I don't have an answer. I turned, pushed my way through some future witnesses. Maybe I should have been there for my mates. They are, were, as good as me. I'm no more worth saving than any of them. A month ago I would've joined in. Now it happens in a blur, and I walk away, unrecognised, anonymous in the crowd.

Kyle got five years for concealed carry plus GBH, and a large scar across his lip where his own knife was used against him. Poor Dildo got ten months and his first ASBO. Danny and Limbo did community service. Troy and the other lad, a guy called Ryan, because they were adult at the time of the offence, got eighteen months each for inciting riots and possession of cannabis, respectively. Fez was stabbed in the stomach by Kyle, and in the chest by a guy I know vaguely as Cappo, and succumbed to his wounds four hours later in the care of Sandford General Hospital, watched over by his mother, Mary Ann Freeman. That was how the paper put it.

I don't think about Rainbow much that September. We spend all our time on the beach, me and Ash, Mike and Jamie, and a new mate called Squidy, enjoying the freedom of no longer being in education. Only Mike gets high enough grades to go to college, and he starts to flunk as soon as he gets there, dragged down by us, no doubt, calling him out to play. I dig out my old wetsuit and learn to surf properly. I pass my test, buy a car and work as a driver for a kebab house. I crack jokes, life stays busy, I get by. Then when the seasons start to change and winter comes, I think about her. How she tasted of strawberry lip balm and hot chocolate in the cold nights of early summer on the coast. How the way she looked at me when she was disappointed and expected more had almost a cruelty about it, a look of pain and self-control and knowledge hardened into stone that hinted at things she had been through, things she had had to leave behind. I suppose it took those few months of living, of not thinking of her, for the shock to wear off. For me to understand something I still can't articulate about loss. After that winter I tried to put her out of my mind, but I think of her again the next April, around the time we met, and the next, and then all the summers since, 'til I'm a lot older and maybe not at all wiser. I guess some girls just stand out more than the others.

And you. Yes, you. You thought this was just some book – a fairytale about a mildly hard-up kid from up north with a twist at the end. Well, this isn't. It fucking isn't. It's my life and I have to live it. And it doesn't just stop because this book is over.

There's no underlying reason for why I am who I am, why my life has happened how it has. I am not gay and frustrated. I was not abused at twelve by an evil PE teacher. I am not neglected, or unloved. Equally, at the end of this story, I do not die of an overdose, Rainbow is not revealed to be my long lost twin, neither of us kill ourselves. I am just a boy, a man, a man/boy, a teenager . . . I'm a human being, in any case. Perhaps I had a crap education, perhaps I fell in with the wrong crowd, perhaps I am ever so slightly emotionally malnourished. Maybe, but there will be no equal, opposing force to balance this out and deliver a happy ending. These flaws and mistakes and missed chances will not be redeemed. Rainbow does not come running back at the last moment, eyes bright, breasts heaving, and Flick confesses his deepest feelings. No. Our lovers lose each other in the dense, chaotic and impossible matter of living. Two arrows flying through the dark and missing each other, maybe by a fraction of an inch.

Think of that person you knew when you were a kid, who you always thought you could have loved completely and forever. Well, you could have. It's the truth, and it's the saddest and simplest thing. There isn't just one person for each of us in the world. There aren't many, but there are always a few people we could have made it with, that maybe we still want to make it with, that press themselves so close to our hearts they leave scars, and then slip through our fingers and disappear from our lives. And it doesn't make a difference if you're thirteen or ninety-eight because some things you feel are real, no matter when. Yes. I could have loved Rainbow forever. Yes. I could have had a better life. Yes. I could have been lifted from poverty and hopelessness and total, mind-rotting boredom.

But I will not be. I may never be. Because this is not the story of a faceless teenage down-and-out. It is my life. And unlike the pages of a flick-book – a series of fast and frenetic images, delivered in double time, a bit of humour, a dash of tragedy, fairly black and white in its lack of variety, each page a story, each flick a life failing – it will not end when the pages run out. Only this book will.

So. Life goes on and I don't really expect much from it. Try not to think about it/her/him, enjoy what you can, and turn the page. FLICK.

blog and newsletter

For literary discussion, author insight,
book news, exclusive content,
recipes and giveaways, visit the
Weidenfeld & Nicolson blog and
sign up for the newsletter at:

www.wnblog.co.uk

For breaking news, reviews and exclusive competitions
Follow us 🐦 @wnbooks
Find us 📘 facebook.com/WNfiction